Unwrap
My
HEART

Alex Falcone | Ezra Fox

Completely
Legitimate
Publishing

Acknowledgements

To Chris Smith, Caitlin Kunkel, and Molly Elwood for reading this book when it was a less good book. To Megan Falcone, Theresa Falcone, Tanya Smith, and Bill Cernansky for reading it when it was a better but still messy book. To Sarah Hatheway for telling us to expand on the phallus part. For Sarah Jebrock and Caleb Fox for nearly everything else.

And for Chris Smith again for helping us come up with the idea.

Cover art by Ryan Alexander-Tanner

ohyesverynice.com

Authors

ALEX FALCONE is comedian, writer, and podcaster living in Portland, OR. He's a regular on the IFC show *Portlandia* and has appeared at numerous comedy festivals including Bridgetown, Bumbershoot, Sketchfest, and the Brooklyn Comedy Festival. He's written for *The Portland Mercury*, *The Willamette Week*, and the public radio show *Live Wire*, and his work has been quoted in *Rolling Stone*, *VOX*, *Boing Boing*, and been featured on the front page of *Reddit*. AND he once got an ice cream named after him.

Despite these modest accomplishments, he somehow remains totally down to earth and approachable.

EZRA FOX was too busy to send me a bio when I asked, so I've elected to invent one for him.

Ezra is a writer, father, river guide, estranged congressman, and sub-par starfighter from the Andromeda galaxy. His skills include Japanese paper folding, knife combat, precision diving, stage illusions, pan flute, sub-par starfighting, and diplomacy.

A terrible car accident in 2007 left him without a conscience or follow-through, so he spends his days tracking down people he perceives to have wronged him and then failing to enact revenge.

This is not his first novel.

READ IT AND WEEP is a podcast about books, movies, and TV that Alex and Ezra host along with Chris and Tanya Smith. This idea was conceived on that show. If, for some reason, you haven't listened yet, you should do that.

read-weep.com

Published by Completely Legitimate Publishing
a division of AGB International
a division of Sesame Pete

CATALOG DATA
Authors: Falcone, Alex
Fox, Ezra
Unwrap My Heart (or It's Time For Mummies!)
ISBN: 978-0-9983611-0-9
Categories: 1. Young adult fiction. 2. Fantasy.
3. Romance. 4. Mummies. 5. Inside jokes taken too far.

Book design by Alex Falcone

completelylegitimatepublishing.com

10 9 8 7 6 5 4 3 2 1

For our Meat Buddies

"There's little joy in life for me,
	And little terror in the grave;
I've lived the parting hour to see
	Of one I would have died to save."
- Charlotte Brontë

Prologue

He wanted everybody to call him "The Priest" even though his real name was Harold. Maybe *because* his name was Harold.

He readied a series of small mason jars on a workbench in the dusty tomb we were sharing at the moment. They were too new, the jars. Like he got them from IKEA so he could pretend he was into canning, but it was obvious this was their first use.

Do they even have IKEA in Egypt? Do evil priests go to chain furniture stores? Do they like meatballs? Mmm, meatballs.

Great, in addition to the discomfort of being tied to an old chair in preparation for ritual sacrifice, now I was hungry.

The Priest sharpened a ceremonial knife with a carved ivory handle. Of course this asshole still buys ivory.

I didn't want to die, obviously, but I tried to look on the bright side: my death would save the people I loved the most, Dad, Mom, Duncan, and *him*. Him. I loved him, I knew that now.

Plus I wouldn't have to go to Trig on Monday.

Chapter 1

I was having an averagely bad Thursday. You know the kind, if you were to draw a Venn diagram of days with "school-related mistakes" and "social mistakes", today would be dead center.

The school mistake was forgetting to finish my essay about South American exports for geography; the social one was spilling a large amount of salsa on my shirt from my giant plate of lunch nachos.

"You should have seen the other guy," I told my friend, Duncan.

"You mean the nachos?"

"Yeah. At least I wasn't eaten by an uncoordinated giant."

I sat in the cafeteria thinking about other Venn diagrams today could fit into ("Was this shirt even clean to begin with?" and "Am I the only one who doesn't care about the sports thing that happened last night?") when he walked in.

Before I tell you about him, it's important that you know I don't do this kind of thing all the time. I never do it.

I almost never do it.

The people sitting at other tables seemed unfazed by the presence of this startlingly handsome new student. I was immediately fazed.

He fit in the middle of a Venn diagram titled "Attributes Sofia Finds Hot". The circles included

- Skinny
- Mysterious
- Confident
- Well dressed

  And

- Miscellaneous hotness catch-all category

He was *really* skinny. Clearly not much for sports. He looked like he was built for drinking coffee and having opinions about music. He had these long elegant fingers, wrapped in these thin gloves, that rested peacefully on the table next to his tray as he stared off into space for a moment.

Despite the tray, he had no food. That was already weird enough, but he was also wearing a hoodie, which wasn't very common since it was too hot in Rock Ridge to ever wear sweatshirts. Even the winter was shorts weather most days.

He took out his phone and started reading something.

As I contemplated this odd behavior, I noticed that even from across the room he had the darkest eyes. They were inset so far that with the shadows from his hoodie, you couldn't even tell if he *had* eyes at all. And yet there was something enchanting about those voids. I could stare into the blank space where his eyes should be all day, and I would, if I hadn't had a terrible realization.

If I could see his eye-areas, he must be looking back at me.

Oh, God.

Quickly I looked away like I was a puppy interested in everything around me. Sure, I was staring at you, but now I'm staring at this poster about Kate running for Student Body President. Now I'm staring at the air conditioning vent. I stare at everything, not just the new hot guy. I'm just a starer. Nothing weird about at that.

While I continued my charade, I could feel his gaze on the back of my neck and I shivered slightly.

Rock Ridge was a small high school, but the cafeteria was particularly tiny, maybe 15 tables total. Since there wasn't room for everybody, we were allowed to eat lunch outside (if you could find sufficient shade) or off campus.

Obviously the choice between driving with friends to a local fast food place or sitting in the stuffy school cafeteria was a no brainer, so the kids who stayed tended to be the underclassmen and the under-cool ones. I tended to be in the latter category anyway, but I stayed because my dad didn't think it was safe to leave school property in the middle of the day.

Duncan stayed because he wanted to keep me company. His dad didn't stop him from driving anywhere he wanted, but he chose to eat with me, which was very generous.

"What's with the new kid?" Duncan asked, amused. "He's staring at us like we're the weirdos. But what is *he* wearing?"

I admit it was strange. The hoodie, the flowy pants, and the gloves that kinda looked like bandages, all of them a cream color. The kids at Rock Ridge tended to favor jeans and graphic tees. Yet there was a confidence about how different he looked; like he wouldn't even get mad if he heard Duncan making fun of him.

Not that Duncan's mean. He's a teddy bear, if instead of being cuddly, a teddy bear was huge, muscle-y, and outgoing. He played baseball and had really bulked up these last couple years. Everyone who met Duncan liked him already, but the muscles had changed the way girls looked at him. They would follow him around between classes and stand around with him giggling at everything he said.

For some reason he seemed oblivious to their affection and prefered to hang out with me. I assumed it was because he was afraid of them and I was safe, you know? We'd known each other since we were kids, so even though it sounds trite, we were like brother and sister.

I think I can do better than that. It was like if you had a pet pig and you liked that little guy so much you sometimes forgot that pigs are usually considered food. You might even eat bacon in front of him, not meaning to offend him but just because you don't think of him that way.

Hrm. Now it's starting to sound mean. I meant that I'm the pig in this metaphor. And seriously, if Duncan wanted to eat ham in front of me, that'd be fine. We're just really good friends. Really good friends who compare each other to pigs.

I'm making this worse, aren't I?

We were like brother and sister.

I stared at the new kid again. He was back to his phone, and I noticed that oddly he wasn't using his fingers to browse it but was using some kind of stylus. Another odd thing. Maybe he was an artist? He caught me looking again and smiled at me. I shivered.

Jeez. Why was I staring at him so much? More importantly, why was he staring back? Even in this losers den of a cafeteria, I wasn't the most attractive girl by a long shot.

Not that I'm unattractive, but neither is the color beige or the word "satisfactory" or the number 6. Nobody asks out the number 6, even if she's got a great sense of humor.

I should probably describe myself better than that, but ugh, I don't want to.

Fine, I'll give it a try. I have painfully straight brown hair that I usually keep just above my shoulders. I've never been much for makeup. Well, every once in awhile I go through a phase where I buy some and try it for a day or two but then give up. I wear glasses. I don't know. What else? My face is rounded but my body is boxy? I look like a basketball on a big box on two longer boxes. And the basketball is wearing glasses.

Ugh, it's so much easier describing other people.

Oh, I know. Do you want a list of my five least favorite features? That I can do no problem. My calves are too big. There's this space between my top two front teeth and the ones next to them on the right side that has always bothered me. I always close my eyes in photos, which maybe isn't a feature exactly but if you only saw photos of me you'd think I was like 80% eyelid. While we're in that area, my eyelashes are too short. Not like freakishly short but I've always wished I had beautiful long lashes. And I'm too pale. Boom. Described.

Maybe those seem a bit nitpicky, but who hasn't sat around nitpicking about their appearance? And you're the one who wanted to know what I look like for some reason. This is on you.

"Hey, Princess Sofia? You still with me? You're making us both look bad here."

"I'm sorry, Dunc. You're right. It's weird. He looks... weird."

"Whatever. Obviously you're in love with him, and you

don't want to talk about it. Be sure to invite me to your wedding."

I smacked Duncan's block of an arm. I'm sure I'm never getting married, but if I did, I'd make him my maid of honor for sure. I wouldn't ask him to find a size 28 dress, but I'd want him by my side, and he'd be great at planning a bachelorette party.

We met when I was 8 or 9 when my dad backed our Subaru into his parents' minivan in the parking lot of a Rascal's. While they were fighting over who was at fault, they realized they had lots in common. Fishing, bowling, the Dodgers, and ice cream.

While we were standing in the parking lot being mortified by the argument-turned-bromance, Duncan and I realized we also had lots in common. Mainly not caring about fishing, bowling, and anybody who dodges anything. We were in favor of ice cream, but that's a pretty basic connection.

We'd been inseparable ever since, even when puberty hit one of us like a ton of testosterone-filled bricks. He tripled in size and I remained a constant size of box.

"So how about it? Will your dad let you go camping with us this weekend?"

Rock Ridge is a couple hours outside LA, but far enough to feel like it's another world. The city is completely surrounded by desert mountains, which makes it easy to feel trapped and, especially with the hot and dry climate, like you're living in a giant pothole.

For people who like small town life, hiking, camping, and Native American artifacts, it was great. Also available: sudden dust storms, weird bunkers from old military tests, and a very short drive to Death Valley, if you really hated being comfortable.

I loved the dry heat, but it's a terrible place to live if you like doing things on the weekends.

I especially didn't like camping, since there's extra dirt and no internet access. Duncan's family loved it, and he'd been bugging me to tag along with them on this trip for months. I'd remained non-committal up until now, which was pretty much the last moment.

"It'll be so great. We could survey the grounds near the cave I found last time. This summer I'm going to apply for a permit to excavate it for Coso artifacts."

Forgot to mention: in addition to his mainstream hobbies of camping and baseball, Duncan was a muscle-y teddy bear who loved archaeology. So not really like a teddy bear at all. Maybe I'm not great at describing other people either.

Though I couldn't care less about archeology, let me brag on my Duncan for just a second. He was pretty famous for his digging. He was the youngest person to publish a scholarly paper on native people in the southwestern US. He specialized in the Coso people, the native tribe that lived in this area before there was enough air conditioning to make it half tolerable. It's highly illegal to disturb artifacts from indigenous people, but Duncan was one of 4 people in the state to get special dispensation from the tribe to excavate on their behalf, and the only one who wasn't a Ph.D. So yeah, very cool if you're into that sort of thing, which I sometimes pretend to be to make Duncan happy.

"I'll let you know," I said. "My dad doesn't like the idea of his best friend and his daughter driving in an RV together. It's like the nuclear codes or the recipe for Coke. If we crash, he's out the only two people he likes in the entire world."

"It's plenty safe. I'll have my dad call him."

"I don't know."

The bell rang, and a collective grumble rose from the

cafeteria. I couldn't argue with the masses. If there was one thing I hated more than geography, it was geography on a day when I forgot to do my homework.

"I'll let you know, Dunc. No promises."

Duncan made puppy dog eyes at me. A muscly amateur archaeologist teddy bear with puppy dog eyes. Is he getting harder to picture every time I describe him? I'm so sorry.

I smacked him. "Stop it. You know I can't say no when you look at me like that."

His eyes took up half his face, and his lip quivered.

"Too far. Now you just look pathetic. See you after geo."

"Try not to get married to that new kid."

"Try not to shut up, Duncan! Or, you know, try to actually shut up. GAH!"

Flustered, I looked for the new kid but he was gone. In his place, there was a small cloud of dust. It was impossible for me to already miss staring at him, right?

I headed to class, wondering if maybe this was a much worse Thursday than I originally thought.

Despite being small, Rock Ridge High was made up of about six buildings with covered concrete paths between them all and occasional clumps of sagebrush dotting the otherwise barren ground between brick buildings. Land was so cheap in this area, they seemed to want to show off by spreading everything out as much as possible. Teachers said the layout was designed to make it feel more like college to prepare us for the future, but mostly it just made it easier to be late for class, and everybody showed up glistening with sweat.

I walked slowly and searched the small clusters of students for the new guy but didn't see him. Everybody was walking in twos and threes, but since Duncan was my only friend and he was headed the opposite direction, I was on my own. I took my time, pulling out my phone and pretending to check for messages. I swiped aimlessly then gave up and made a note to figure out an excuse to get out of camping.

I made another note to draw up these hilarious Venn diagrams I'd been imagining. And to research thin flowing hoodies. And to find this new guy on Instagram and go through all his pictures in the middle of the night. I deleted that note just in case I got hit by a car on the way home and the authorities went through my phone, but I filed it away mentally because I was definitely going to do it.

Chapter 2

I would still have been thinking about the new kid all through geography even if he hadn't walked in five minutes late and sat down next to me. His intriguing clothing hid the perspiration the rest of us were still wiping away. Maybe that's why he did it?

As soon as he slid into the desk next to mine, the one that had been recently abandoned when Amanda Spitz moved away, I knew there was zero chance I'd be paying attention to Mr. Graff today.

I immediately noticed that he smelled intoxicating. Exotic oils of some kind, mixed with that clean scent of a desert evening after a summer rain. Something about his presence made me sit up straighter and dread washed over me when I remembered the nacho stain on my shirt. I squirmed, trying to sit in a way that hid it from his view.

"Everybody, this is Seth," Mr. Graff said, pointing at the Desert Rain Smell, who looked down shyly. "He just transferred here from, was it Atlanta?"

Rain Smell nodded.

"This is our first transfer from Atlanta and since we haven't sent anybody there, you could say we have a trade deficit with the good people of Georgia."

Mr. Graff surveyed the class, beaming.

"That was a joke. Geez, lighten up everybody. I was on Leno, remember?"

He waited for somebody to ask him about it but he got nothing. When it was clear he wasn't going to get any audience participation, he launched into the story anyway.

"It was 1993. November 17th. Bulgaria had just defeated France in the World Cup qualifier, and Leno had me on to do this trick where I juggled ketchup bottles and prepared hot dogs at the same time...."

Nobody was listening. Instead the whole class was sneaking glances at Seth and, by extension, me. I didn't dare look over; staring was a range weapon and we were in very close quarters. This was more smelling distance.

I needed to wait until he was absorbed in an assignment and then I could put in some good glancing time, which is as good as I could do from this range.

"So I said to Jay, 'I'm not saying Bill Clinton gets around, but at the White House they're calling him Emil Kostadinov." Mr. Graff paused for a laugh that wouldn't come.

"The Bulgarian football star, " he added. "Get it? Because he scored so much? It was risque but it killed at the time."

Seth gave a sympathetic chuckle because he was new and probably felt guilty. The rest of us had heard enough about Mr. Graff's performing past to feel no guilt about anything. Hearing the laugh, Mr. Graff smiled to himself.

"Still got it," he murmured.

Maybe with all that reminiscing, he'd forget about the essays we were supposed to turn in--

"Now I trust you all have the essays that were due today?"

Crap. I wasn't usually the type to space on a homework assignment, but recently I had developed a debilitating on-line genealogy habit. Several hours a day. It wasn't going to make for the sexiest intervention, but in my defense, nothing in health class warned us of the addictive properties of Ancestry.com.

Instead of going to parties or football games, I combed through ship manifests from the 1800s, chasing that first high of discovering my great grandmother's maiden name. It was Grunkle. Great Grandma Agnes Grunkle. Actually, I can see why she might've wanted it lost to the sands of time.

If I'm being honest, I thought that if I could figure out my mom's family tree, it would explain why she had run off when I was 10. Like maybe everybody in her family split when they hit 40. So far, I hadn't proven that hypothesis, but I hadn't disproven it either.

Plan B was to find the family she might've run to. I liked to think it was a healthy addiction. Y'know, like hummus or exercise. And as the saying goes, knowledge is power and power brings back the people who ripped a hole in your life by running away. That's a saying, right? Or maybe it's "Don't look at a horse's mouth." I'm bad with sayings.

It didn't matter what I was doing because, while I had researched and even outlined my paper on South American exports, I hadn't actually gotten around to writing it, and now I was screwed.

"I want you to turn to your table-mate and start discussing your essays. Focus on the political implications of changing export climates. Table-mates, ask tough questions!"

What? No. I couldn't just talk to this guy face to face. He was a 10. 10s are for admiring creepily across the lunchroom and subtly smelling in class. You don't just talk to them. I was having enough trouble focusing with him so close.

I turned my body mechanically toward him but didn't look up.

"I'm Seth."

"The import. Yeah, I know," I said in the general direction of his desk.

"That's right. And you are?"

"Oh right. I'm Sofia, I guess."

"You guess?"

"I'm like 80% sure at this point."

"Sofia." He said it slowly like he was tasting each of the syllables, deciding if he liked them. "Isn't there a Princess Sofia? Sweden, I think?"

"Oh great, you know things too."

"What?"

"Oh geez. Nothing. I don't know. Well, this is my stop," I said, and got up to leave.

He chuckled. "Don't go. I don't know why that's the first thing I thought of. Sofia just sounds like a princess name to me. Maybe there's a Disney princess named Sofia."

"There is, but it sounds less princessy when I say the whole thing. Sofia Murdoch. Princess Murdoch? Never. Too businessy. Lord Murdoch, sure. Or Chief Technology Officer Murdoch. Or Captain Murdoch. Really anything but princess."

"Fair point. I guess I'll have to stick to just the first name then, Princess Sofia."

For reasons I can't fully explain, everybody had been calling me princess since I was a little girl. When my Duncan or my dad says it, it's sweet. From some people, it feels mean. Now this? I'd have to consider more, but initially it seemed like a bit of both. Maybe playfully mean.

"Since I just got here, I guess you'll have to tell me

about your essay. Don't worry, my questions will be tough, but fair."

"You're out of luck, because I didn't finish. I got distracted."

He leaned in conspiratorially and his face elongated like he was raising an eyebrow but it was hidden by his hoodie. "By what?"

He wasn't lying about tough but fair. But no. There was no way I'd let my obsession with old marriage licenses and sepia photos of dead people slip to this attractive new boy.

He could torture me all he wanted but I'd never reveal my secret. He'd run screaming from the room when he found out how weird my hobbies were. Brain, time to think of a lie. Make it a good one so he thinks you're cool.

"I found an obituary for my great great uncle in New Orleans. He got run over by a bus."

Well shit. Mouth, were you even listening to Brain? Brain, why did you let Mouth get away with that? We need to present a unified front here, guys! Get it together, you're making us all look bad.

I braced myself for his befuddled indifference to my revelation.

"Really?" He propped his head on his begloved knuckles. "That's pretty cool."

You see, Mouth, this is why we need to have more meetings, you're always running off and... wait, what?

"You're kidding, right? Or did I miss the sarcasm? Do they do sarcasm differently in Atlanta?"

"Seriously! I love learning about distant family members. I was adopted but I did lots of research about my birth family."

I searched his face. He didn't look like this was an elaborate hoax. He just opened up to me. Was... was I nailing this? Go, Beige, go!

"I thought I was the only one who cared about genealogy," I said.

"No, it's fascinating. It's this weird little window to the past. Very foggy, since record keeping was so shoddy, but every once in awhile you get this very clear glimpse at somebody who has a lot to teach you about how you got here."

"You're not kidding. I wish it wasn't so shoddy so the glimpses could be bigger. I mean, for once I'd like to see a ship's manifest where the first mate had legible handwriting." I said, rolling my eyes.

"Right? Did they only write stuff down during storms?"

"I KNOW!"

He laughed and shook his head, which made absolutely no sense. It was a real laugh, too. Not that sympathy chuckle he gave Mr. Graff.

All I wanted was to hear him laugh that magical laugh again. It sounded like wind chimes, but deep and sexy wind chimes. Wind chimes I would totally go to town on. I don't know what I'm saying anymore.

I changed my mind. Today's Venn diagram just switched to "Most surreal conversations ever" overlapped with "Definitely a good day and getting better every minute". And much smaller at the bottom, still a circle for spilling salsa on myself.

That thought, of course, jinxed it. Mr. Graff interrupted this weird, brilliant moment.

"Now class, hang onto your essays because they're going to be the starting point for the group project. In the teams of two you're in right now"—WE'RE A TEAM! I MIGHT DIE.—"you're going to be creating a presentation on the region you were assigned." He grabbed an imaginary microphone for a Leno impression. I think. He's terrible at impressions, and I never actually watched Leno.

"Princess Sofia!"

I definitely didn't like it from Mr. Graff. "Yeah?"

"Since Seth doesn't have an essay, you'll both be working from yours. Unless you want to switch to the Middle East, since that's the region Seth would have been assigned. But then all the work you did on your own essay will have gone to waste."

"Sounds good!"

"Really?" Mr. Graff seemed shocked but Seth jumped in.

"I hate to waste Sofia's great work on her first essay, but it'd be really interesting to write about the Middle East," he said, and winked at me. Or at least I think it was a wink. He had such deep set eyes it was kinda hard to tell. HE MIGHT HAVE WINKED AT ME. STILL THINKING ABOUT DYING. LUNGS, SLOW IT DOWN A BIT.

"Um, that's fine with me. We'll go with what Seth wants, since he's new."

"Great," said Mr Graff. "Challenge yourselves, I like it. You're going to be a couple of regular Emil Kostadinovs."

Nobody laughed.

Challenge was an understatement. I'd just agreed to work on a group project with the hottest guy I'd ever laid eyes on. Maybe the hottest guy eyes had ever been laid upon, period. Eyes burn up on contact with this guy, he's so hot, and those eyes die happy.

"You'll need to give a 15-minute presentation on Monday. I'll give you the rest of the class to figure out what you're going to do, but you'll definitely have to meet over the weekend as well. Be sure to start with an outline..."

I stopped listening because my head was spinning. I realized that every wink comes at a price from the universe. As relieved as I was to not have to go camping, having to tell Duncan I couldn't go was going to straight up ruin his day. That's going to be one sad, muscly, amateur archeologist teddy—y'know, let's just call him a dude. One sad dude.

Seth leaned over again, and I caught a whiff of his dusty fragrance. I forgot about Duncan. Duncan who? No, Officer, I've never even heard the name Duncan before.

"Since you didn't do the essay, I thought it would help if we switched topics," he whispered. "You're my first friend here, so I want to get on your good side."

I think I said something vaguely affirmative. "Glurg," maybe.

"Plus, I know a ton about Egypt so that'll make it easier. That's where my birth family is from so all my genealogy might come in handy."

"Oh, very very glurg!" My voice came back about half way. Even though I felt bad for Duncan, it was hard to stay upset when I could be learning about Seth's ancestry. I mean, any ancestry's good, but *Seth's* ancestry. That's, like, the hottest ancestry. Ugh, I'm the worst.

"Do you talk to them? Can we just ask them to write this for us?"

"They're all dead now."

Oh, good move, Beige. Make this moment a huge bummer.

"Oh no, I'm so sorry."

"Look, I'm sorry I brought it up. I don't like to talk about my family. It's ancient history."

Mouth, this is Brain. I'm getting some weird readings on this one. Let's take it easy. Make him laugh again so we can hear those deep, sexy wind chimes.

"I had a second cousin once removed who was exiled from Moldova for gerrymandering. And a great grandmother named Grunkle. That's a crime in itself."

He smiled, but he still looked sad. Moderate success, Mouth/Brain. One more and we've got this. Make it a good one.

"Your family is from Egypt, and they're ancient history. Are they sphinxes?" I dropped my voice conspiratorially. "Did they die from embarrassment about the nose job?"

B+ on that one, team. But you tried. Mr. Graff would be proud.

He didn't laugh. He looked down, hurt. Oh God, no. I had it, and then I lost it. I always do this. No, no no no no.

"Oh god, I'm so sorry. I was trying to be funny. That wasn't racist, was it? This always happens."

"Don't worry about it," he mumbled just as the bell rang. He grabbed his books, and before I knew what was happening, he was out the door.

The love of my life was opening up to me about gene-alogy, and then I said something racist, and he was gone.

I was right earlier when I said I might die. I should have specified I'll die alone.

Chapter 3

That night I was still thinking about Seth when I smelled charcoal and heard the smoke alarm going off, then the beep of somebody pressing the "it's okay" button.

"Who wants my famous Friday Night Pancakes?" Dad burst through my bedroom door wearing an apron and holding a smoking skillet. I wiped my eyes and shut my laptop.

"Dad, I'm 17. I don't get sad on Friday nights anymore," I lied.

He looked at me like he knew better, but mercifully didn't correct me.

"So I guess you don't want your pop's burnt pancakes?" he asked. His mustache twitched, and he sniffed, really hamming it up.

"No, I *want* them. I just want you to know I don't *need* them," I said.

"Good. Because a grown man eating burnt flapjacks alone on a Friday night is just about the saddest thing I've ever heard of."

"Well, we can't have that," I said. I took my cat from my

lap and plopped him on top of my warm computer. "Stay, Bastian. I won't be long."

Remind me to tell you more about him later, because Bastian is the greatest. But real quick: he has this long brown hair that makes him look like an insane physicist or a sane symphony conductor.

Like most cats, he's a narcoleptic sociopath, so he ignored me and was asleep before I left the room.

We ate at the counter—the table was too big for the two of us so we rarely used it. When we finished, Dad smiled down at me.

"It was 102 today," he said brightly.

"Oh?" I pretended not to know where he was going with this.

"I only mention it because *I* said it would be 102. You made the good-natured but ultimately incorrect guess of 99 degrees, well below average for this time of year."

"Murmph," I said through pancake.

"Murmph, indeed, Princess Sofia," he said, getting up and patting his belly. "And your loyal subjects thank you in advance for doing the dishes."

"I always do the dishes," I mumbled.

"Then you should know better than to bet on dish duty with the weatherman."

"We live in the desert, Dad. Weatherman's the easiest job ever."

"And yet I'm so much better at it than you," he said.

"You also have access to a lot of equipment, whereas I'm just guessing."

"True. But you knew that when you made the bet."

"When's the last time you predicted rain?"

"April Fools' Day two years ago."

"You see?" I stood up, decisive. "Tomorrow I bet it's 101."

He sighed at me, the way he sighs when Bastian knocks over her food bowl. Like, "It's not your fault you are what you are." That kind of sigh.

"And you even say this when it's clearly going to be a scorching 104."

I trudged over to the sink and started scrubbing. I think he knew something was up because I actually did a good job cleaning the pan. Normally I wash and he dries, and he's the kind of supportive dad who just doesn't send anything back for a re-scrubbing. If it's still dirty, then he'll clean it with the towel.

"So Hank called me about the camping trip this weekend," he said.

"Oh, well actually--"

"And I figured, what the hell, you deserve it."

"What? Really?"

Dad reached behind the table and pulled a brand new sleeping bag from a shopping bag on the floor. "Stopped on the way home and got you this. Weatherman says it's going to drop below 40 at night."

"That's sweet of the weatherman to think of me, but it turns out I can't go."

"No, I just told you you can," he said, confused. "I'm your dad. That's how permission works." He raised an eyebrow. "Do you have an even stricter dad that I don't know about? We should have weekly meetings, him and I. Get on the same page."

"I can't go because Mr. Graff gave me a group project with this moody new kid, and I have to work on it over the weekend."

"Ah. School Dad told you that? He's worse than Strict Dad. Probably should listen to him."

"I don't care for School Dad," I said.

"Now sweetie, he's more afraid of you than you are of him. Do you want to bring the moody new kid here or have him meet you at a neutral location?"

"I'll text him and divvy up the work. No one needs to meet face to face anymore."

"Sure, sure. Is the new kid a boy? A girl? A sexy boy?" He gauged my response, and I tried to keep a neutral face.

"Just a boy," I lied.

"Uh huh. Well, just remember what I always say--"

"Yeah, I know: 'Spare the Mace, spoil the boyfriend'."

"That's right. You kiss whoever you want, but if someone does something you don't like, you get to Macing right quick. Of course, you'll have to be face to face for that. 'Face to face is the place for Mace,' I always say."

"I know, Dad. You say that a lot. Even when it's not really applicable."

"It's always applicable."

"Dad, we're just working on a geography paper. Sometimes I think you want to solve all your problems with Mace."

"Show me a problem that can't be Maced, and I'll show you a mugger with goggles," he said, then kissed me on the forehead and went to watch VHS tapes of classic bowling championships.

"I don't even know what that means!" I yelled after him.

My dad was tall with strong arms from pointing at maps that don't exist and a contagious smile, protected from the elements by a thick umbrella of a mustache that he'd been cultivating since college, now flecked with grey. His curly black hair was cut short and receding just a bit and also slightly greying at the sideburns, but because of the smile, the changes in his hair never seemed to bother him; he just looked more confident as it changed. He was so confident in his aging it almost seemed like he was always supposed to be 50 and was just now getting around to it.

Also worth mentioning about him: He had taken care of me nearly flawlessly since my mom left us. And after he watched an episode of *Nightline* about salmonella like 10 years ago, he was strongly against undercooking food. Or cooking it a normal amount.

These last two things are connected, I guess. He's sometimes very protective of me (see overcooking food and his obsession with pepper spray), but he's also oddly fair. He doesn't like me walking anywhere alone after 4pm or driving with people he hasn't pre-approved, but making terrible, life-altering mistakes would be fine as long as I learned from them.

He said I got a single "$100 screw-up" every three months, though I rarely needed to cash them in. A couple times I'd taken the fall for something Duncan did, like when he hit our mailbox backing out of our driveway, and I pretended I had done it.

I can only hope Duncan doesn't get some girl pregnant, because I'll have a heckuva time taking the fall for that one.

Dad didn't talk about Mom much except when I brought her up, which I did from time to time.

"Aren't you pissed she left?" I'd say.

"Some days? Absolutely," he'd say. "But other days I think she must've had a good reason to leave you behind, Princess. She loved you more than pie."

"And that was a lot?"

"Oh yeah."

After putting it off all night, I called up Duncan to break the news that I wouldn't be going with him on the big camping trip. The big guy was not going to like this. There should be a law against making Duncan sad. He sounds like a big teddy bear who found out he's going to be incinerated because he's been contaminated with scarlet fever. Sorry I couldn't think of a more topical reference but I'm really trying to run with this teddy bear thing.

The real problem was that he never wanted anyone to feel bad, so he would stay really positive the whole time. One time I accidentally bent his autographed Ken Griffey Jr. rookie card while doing my famous "Baseball Card Puppet Show."

"No problem," he had managed between sniffles. "The show must go on."

If he would just get angry, it'd be much easier on me.

He picked up on the first ring and as soon as I heard his voice I wished I'd just taken the cowardly way out and texted him.

"Heya Princess. You called to discuss the finer points of s'mores technique?"

"No, because there's only one technique. You burn it to crap so you don't get salmonella and then try not to catch your mouth on fire."

"Your dad must be very proud."

"Charcoal's a vital nutrient, Dunc. If you had gotten more of it, your growth might not've been so stunted."

"Well, lucky for you I bought us an extra large tent to share on the trip. No more of this, 'you-hogging-all-the-space' that always seems to happen, Gigantor," said Duncan.

"Yeah, about that..." I started.

"But honestly, I'm really happy you can come. I'm just miserable when you're not there." He paused. "You know what I'm trying to say, right Sofia?"

"Sure," I said. "I get lonely sometimes too. I'm glad we're friends. But Duncan--"

"It's more than that, Sof. It's... well, we can talk about it on the trip."

"I can't come on the trip, Dunc." I said.

Then in the pause when all I could hear was Duncan's condemned teddy bear breathing, I added, "I'm really sorry."

"Oh. No biggie."

It'd be so much easier if he'd just explode or cry or something.

"It's all Mr. Graff's fault," I said quickly. "He dumped this project on me with the new kid, so--"

"Wait, you're going to be hanging out with the new kid this weekend instead of me?"

"Not hanging out. I'll probably just end up working alone on it," I said. "Seth doesn't seem to like me much."

"It has a name?" he asked. "I'll remember that for your wedding present."

"He thinks I'm a racist, Duncan! I said the wrong thing. I got tongue-tied with the saliva and all that. I don't know why I was so nervous. Why couldn't it be like talking with you? I don't get nervous talking to you."

"Yeah," said Duncan. "That's weird." In hindsight, this might have been sarcasm but at the moment I mistook it for genuine confusion.

He didn't say anything for a second.

"Duncan, I'm really, really sorry. But you'll do it again, right? And I promise I'll come next time."

"Sure," he said. "Next time I start a major excavation that could change my career." And then he caught himself. "I'm sorry. It sucks you have to spend your weekend on work, Princess."

"Thanks, Seth. So how's--"

"Duncan," he said quietly.

"Sorry?"

"You called me Seth."

"Well, that's super weird of me," I said. "Why would I do that?"

"Charcoal poisoning?" he ventured. Then, clearing his throat, "Might want to cut back."

"Yeah, easier said than done. Did you know Dad burned Corn Flakes yesterday? He decided they might not be toasted well enough at the factory so he--"

"Hey, I actually have to go," he said. "Talk to you later, okay?"

"Oh. Sure thing. Night, Duncan."

"Night, Princess."

I didn't want to think anymore about disappointing Duncan so I needed a distraction right away. There was no way I could focus on the Graff Paper (don't look at me that way; he insisted we call all the work we do for his class Graff Papers. He might have gotten into teaching just for that joke).

I took some video of Bastian to try to make him an internet celebrity. He half-heartedly swiped at my phone and then lazily tried to eat it. Turns out there's a whole genre of cat-eating-phone videos, but to really pull it off well, you have to have another phone recording the whole situation. On the second go around, I tried to get him to eat Dad's phone, but the cat has a healthy respect for my dad and knows better than to mess with his stuff. I posted the video as "Cat stares respectfully at master's cellphone, then loses interest," but it failed to go viral after 45 minutes of constant refreshing so I gave up.

I turned to my ongoing search for the mysteries of my family's darkest secrets and turned up a Great Great Aunt Martha I'd never known about. She was suspected of witchcraft... in 1906. The article was a little light on details, but it looked like her neighbor's horse died in a buggy accident, then the horse's body (allegedly) disappeared, only to (allegedly) appear, bandaged but walking around the next night eating people's carrots from their gardens. When reached for comment, Great Great Aunt Martha said "If I were a witch, wouldn't I just use the power of the universe to make you think I weren't a witch?" I liked her. The reporter did not seem to.

I continued to dig through records and articles, but it wasn't as engrossing as it usually was. In my head, I continually replayed that moment when things were going well with Seth and then I messed it up. I came up with hundreds of better responses and practiced them under my breath.

If Seth thought I was weird when I talked to him, hearing me practice talking to him alone in my room would definitely have made things worse.

I fell asleep at my desk thinking about Seth sitting in the cafeteria looking all hot. I had a dream in which I was slowly unrolling his arm gauze, then I was rudely awoken by Bastian nuzzling my neck.

"Not now, Seth. Not here."

"Meow."

"What?"

"Meow?"

"Oh, God."

"Meow."

"I'm so sorry, Bastian. I thought you were... never mind."

I got ready and settled into my for-real bed and Bastian curled up on my feet. I know eating pancakes with your dad and accidentally having a sexual moment with your cat doesn't seem like a great Friday night, but I've had much worse.

Chapter 4

When I woke up late on Saturday morning, I'd given up on a few things: passing geography, being funny in public, and ever having a boyfriend. I felt the most guilty about the third, since the universe had gone through great lengths to push us together, and in three sentences I'd wrecked all the universe's hard work.

I donned my most somber fluffy bathrobe and prepared myself for a weekend alone working on a presentation I wouldn't be able to give because my partner thought I was racist. I had my slippers on, a cup of hot chocolate steaming in front of me, and my textbooks spread out across the living room floor.

The knock startled me. We didn't get a lot of foot traffic at my dad's house; we lived at the end of an unwelcoming street called Arrowhead Drive. The people who lived on Arrowhead tended towards the reclusive. The whole neighborhood was full of tall stucco-covered walls with big metal rolling gates hiding the often opulent houses from the plebeian public eye.

We hadn't had a trick-or-treater since 2007.

When my parents were first shopping for houses, apparently they'd had a nice long fight about this place. My dad had thought the house looked uninviting from the street and was too far from town, which were both fair points, but my mom had fallen in love with it immediately. It had space to garden, she insisted, though that turned out to be a moot point with the soil here. She had tried diligently anyway, spending most evenings digging in the sand, watering the withering plants and humming to herself.

I gathered my robe around me and cautiously made my way towards our imposing front door. My Mace was all the way upstairs in my backpack, so I carried my cocoa with me in case I needed to defend myself.

"Seth!" I was so surprised I jumped back from the door and spilled cocoa on my robe. I'm lucky it wasn't the Mace.

"I wanted to apologize for what happened in class Friday."

"Um... I accept?" I ventured.

"Good."

We just looked at each other.

"Shouldn't I be the one to apologize?" I asked. "I stayed up late last night writing a good long apology in my head."

"Nope. Can I come in?"

"I guess so."

I closed the door and stood there stupidly with hot chocolate dripping down the front of my robe.

"You're in my house. Why are you in my house?" I was having a lot of trouble believing this was real.

My confusion seemed to shake his confidence, and he wavered slightly.

"I'm sorry. I shouldn't have come." He reached for the door again.

"No, I'm the one who's sorry. I shouldn't have said what I did. Even though I'm not sure why I shouldn't have said it, I'm positive I shouldn't have. And then once I said it, I should have said sorry right away. And then you came here, and I let you say sorry before I got a chance to say sorry, but I should have been the one saying it because it wasn't your fault I said something stupid about sphinxes. I can't figure out why that would upset you since I couldn't find anything on the internet about 'sphinx' being a racial slur or anything, but it clearly upset you because you went from being so happy-seeming to really bummed in an instant. And anyway, I only said it because I wanted you to think I was funny because you dress cool, and you're obviously a 10, but I'm pretty meh looking, so I've got to be fun to hang out with or nobody would even notice me. Not that the sphinx joke was a great example of my amazing sense of humor, because honestly I was a little panicked talking to you, and sometimes when I get nervous I get this thing with saliva, and I tell dad jokes... why am I still talking? I was really expecting you to cut me off somewhere in there."

He was looking at me sideways, and a smile crept onto his face.

"You're doing fine. Keep going. As long as you need."

Was he making fun of me? That's a good sign, right?

"I'm sorry, Seth."

"No, no. I shouldn't be so sensitive. It's just that..."

I gave him what I thought was ample time to finish his sentence. I didn't want to re-ruin everything. We'd been getting along so well these last couple of seconds. Nothing else came out of his perfect mouth.

"Feels like you're missing part of that sentence. Subject, verb, some adjectives. Really the whole thing."

"I grew up in Egypt," he started. "I got teased a lot about stuff like that. There are those terrible movies about, you know, mummies? Kids were brutal."

"I thought there were some fun parts of those movies,"

I offered. "Wasn't The Rock in a couple? I love that guy."

He smiled weakly.

"But seriously, that must have been very hard. Kids are so mean."

"It just reminds me of how much I miss my family, so sometimes I overreact to stuff like that. And I have some especially bad memories that revolve around a sphinx."

"Seth, I'm really sorry," I said quietly.

"It was a long, long time ago. Nothing lasts forever. Definitely not pain."

I tried to change the subject to something safer.

"I was just working on our project if you want to join me. I have to put on some clean clothes. Not that this is clothes, it's a robe. I know that."

He smiled. "I'd love to."

"Is that the moody new kid?" called my dad from the TV room.

I froze like a cat who just heard a dog sniffing under the fence.

"No, no. It's, uh, Seth, my geography partner," I shouted back. I looked at Seth apologetically. "There's this moody new kid in another class," I said to Seth, looking around for help from the inanimate objects in my living room for help. Nothing. "Her name is.... Dar... leen... a. Darleena. Very angsty. I think she's Slovenian. Is that a real thing? Not that I have anything against Slovenians, or anybody for that matter. I'm really not racist at all WHY AREN'T YOU CUTTING ME OFF?"

Seth just shook his head good-naturedly.

"Seth, you wearin' goggles?" yelled my dad.

"Uhm, no? I--"

"Good enough," he said. "Welcome to the Murdoch household. Come in here and let me get a look at you."

Dad was reclined, almost horizontal on the La-Z-Boy. He was watching a bowling tournament he'd DVR'd earlier in the week. Rock Ridge doesn't have its own sports teams, so he'd had to make do with SoCal teams like the Dodgers and Lakers. But his heart was in bowling, "The Game of Kings", he'd say, knowing full well it wasn't.

"You bowl, Seth?"

"I'm no Earl Anthony, but I'm no Tom Daugherty either."

Dad un-reclined his chair so fast he almost folded himself into it. He righted himself, straightened up, and gave Seth a hard stare.

"No goggles and you can name at least two different bowlers? Did you study for this exam?"

Seth ventured a smile. "No sir. Just raised right."

"Pretty good start, young man. How old are you?"

Seth coughed a dry cough. "I'm a junior, sir. Just like Sofia."

"Alright, you can stay," he said. "You don't have reading glasses or any other protective eyewear in that bag of yours?"

Seth shook his head.

"Good boy. You kids play nice," said Dad, and reclined back into oblivion. Seth relaxed visibly.

We weren't the most efficient study partners. I had this plan all worked out: I'd pretend to read but I'd actually stare at him over my book. Then he'd catch me and I'd feel embarrassed so it'd be a while again before I'd work up the courage to try again, but I'd definitely do it. I figured if I played my cards right, I'd get to stare at him for 5, maybe 8 minutes of every hour. And if the other 52-55 minutes I could just smell him, I'd call tonight a success.

If that doesn't sound great, then you just have to take my word for it, because it would have been heavenly.

I'm sorry. I know how this sounds. You have to believe I don't do this all the time. I don't go around finding ways to stare at and smell new boys.

But instead of that awesome plan, something really strange happened. It seemed like—and I don't want to be too braggy here—it seemed like he thought I was cool. That seems like a long shot. Maybe he thought I was so unlikable that I was intriguing? Yeah, that makes more sense.

I'd never been able to talk to guys (except Duncan, of course, but he didn't count). There was something about them that triggered an uncontrollable reaction. You know those people who get dry mouth, sweat profusely, and can't think of anything to say? I *wish* that was my problem. I had the opposite issue, and it was so much worse.

My mouth would fill with saliva, my skin dried out, and then every word I've ever thought tumbled out in a big, wet pile.

It gets worse the hotter the guy is, so with Seth, things were unbearable. Here's a sample:

Seth: Where do you want to start? What part of Egypt are you most interested in?

Me: The camels. They're like horses but scarier. I've been scared of horses since I was 5 when a horse kicked me and broke my arm, and now I can't watch the Kentucky Derby without getting these cold sweats like all these horses are only racing to be the first one to get to me for more kicking. Like they heard I was great to kick and wanted to try for themselves but were worried the others would kick me to death before they got a chance to try it and that's why they're racing. Camels are like that but, obviously, lumpier.

Seth: *Stares at me, but incredibly doesn't run scream-ing from the room.*

He sat unnaturally still, most of the time. Like a doll. And when he thought about something, his mouth tended to hang open. It was cute.

"Okay, let's start by researching the natural resources. I think we can throw camels in there for you, if you aren't too scared."

I shivered.

He continued, "Did you know the British army used camels during the First World War?"

"How would I know that?"

"I don't know. Books?"

"Those are the first drafts of movies, right? Yeah, I've dabbled."

He laughed.

"Obviously early civilizations used them in war too. They've been domesticated for thousands of years."

"This isn't going to take nearly as long as I expected. How about for our presentation you just recite obscure Egyptian facts and I'll cry quietly in the corner?"

"Sounds like a plan, Princess."

"Seriously, you're insanely smart."

He looked down shyly.

"It's just something I'm interested in, especially the dif-ferences between ancient Egypt and the modern country. It's amazing to think it's the same physical place and yet it has so little in common."

He stared into space wistfully, mouth open like a Munch painting. He expounded on the regional differences in agri-cultural production. I typed furiously.

"It's weird, Sofia. I haven't talked this much about my

homeland in years."

"I bet it's hard, because of your family."

"Oh, it is," he said, his deep eyes unfocusing and look-ing somewhere I couldn't see. I reflexively moved to touch his hand. Well, the cloth over his hand. No warmth leaked through his sleeve-glove-things. Man, he dresses weird. Then again, I was the one in the chocolate covered robe. Who was I to judge?

"It shouldn't be," he said, shaking himself awake. "They're happy memories, mostly, but..."

He trailed off. But he didn't move his hand away. I held it there and moved closer to him.

"But those thousand good memories pale in compari-son to the one bad one," I said.

"Yes. That's exactly it."

"That's how I am about my mom too."

"I wasn't going to ask about her because I didn't want to bum you out."

"It's fine," I said. "She left when I was 10. No note. No goodbye. We just woke up one day and she was gone." My voice wasn't shaking, but I felt a single tear trickling down my cheek.

He recoiled a little, like he was worried the tear would jump out and grab him. So he's not big on emotions. Got it. Then he seemed to catch himself and leaned back in.

"Did you ever worry something happened to her?"

"No, she took a single suitcase. Enough for a couple days. A few random things from her room. It seemed clear she wasn't planning on coming back."

"That's so hard. How has your dad handled it?"

"Like a champion."

"He seems like a great guy."

This was starting to feel like... something. But that was

just my imagination. A trick of the light. It was nothing. We... we should go back to the staring and smelling plan. That was safer. Nobody wanted to have a *something* with me when they could have a *nothing*.

I ordered my body to get up and run away. Maybe even grab some pepper spray. But it didn't listen and, much to my horror, my mouth continued without my permission.

"He's pretty great, yeah. But he refuses to talk about it. You're the only person I've told besides Duncan." Seriously, Mouth? We're here with a guy who is trying to comfort us and you bring up another guy? That's it, you're officially fired. We'll get a new spokesperson. Belly Button, what are you up to these days?

"Duncan." He mulled the name over. "He's your big friend."

"Yes. Those words describe him very well. Big. And friend. Kind of like a teddy bear, but then there are all these ways he's not like a teddy bear at all, like his muscles which aren't teddy-like but..."

This time he wisely cut me off.

"So you're not..." He raised his eyebrows to finish the sentence. I think it was his eyebrows.

"No, of course not! I don't have one of those." I said, too fast. Be cool, Sofia. "I hear they're good, though," I added helpfully. "I'm not against it. I'm all for it. But not like creepy all-I-think-about for it. Like, a normal amount for it." GET IN THE GAME, BELLY BUTTON, WE'RE DROWNING UP HERE.

"I don't have one either. I mean, I don't have a girl-friend. In case you were about to ask."

In a million years, I wasn't going to ask that. Or at least, I was going to try to be less obvious, but with this loose cannon mouth, who knows. Was it my turn to say something again? How long had I not responded to him? I swallowed a mouthful of saliva that had materialized in the last milli-second. Let's put together a game plan--

"That's dumb," I blurted.

"What?" He asked, humor in his eyes.

"I mean, it's surprising that a guy like you wouldn't have a girlfriend. The universe is stupid sometimes."

He laughed. "You're pretty surprising yourself. I've never met a girl like you. Ever."

"That's not really a compliment. Or if it is, it's pretty generic."

"Trust me, it is. The greatest, most specific compliment. You're wonderfully unique, Princess Sofia."

"Don't call me that. Only two people can call me that, Duncan and my dad, and only then because they've been grandfathered in. And grandduncaned, in Duncan's case." Oh crap. My dad. He's in the other room, and I have a boy sitting almost on my lap. Confirming he was still alive, my dad yelled something at the TV. I could only make out part of it.

"Ringing 10... too aggressive... wolves are comin'!" Probably not that, but that's as close as I could get.

The tear safely gone from my face, Seth stroked my cheek. "I'm sorry, but Princess just suits you somehow."

"You suit me," I said. NO, WHAT? STOP IT.

Before I could explain away my stupid comment, my mouth got itself in a whole other kind of trouble.

There was a change in the air, like all the particles knew a first kiss was about to happen. Everything got quiet. Behind the scenes, someone threw a blanket over the rest of the world and all I knew was this moment.

Instead of focusing on that, I thought how great it was that I hadn't actually subbed in my belly button because this would be way weirder.

He kissed me like he knew what I meant to say, how I was feeling, how I wanted to feel. I breathed him in. His kiss was confident but not overwhelming. His lips were dry, but perfectly smooth.

When he pulled away, I could hardly breathe. My lungs were suddenly filled with tiny particles of intoxicating dust.

He wiped his mouth with the sleeve of his hoodie. For all I knew this was standard first-kiss behavior, so I mimicked him.

"I'm sorry," I said, woozy.

"For what?" He was laughing again.

"If I wasn't a good kisser. Or if I was, you're welcome."

He kissed me again quickly, and I again found myself trying to catch my breath.

"You were great." He started to get up.

"Are you sure? Because I'm pretty sure I need practice."

He laughed harder.

"I need to go. Your father is going to come in soon, and I don't want him to see us like this. I think we got enough work done for one day. Let's meet up again tomorrow and finish."

"Okay." I took a deep breath then looked up at him. "Is it tomorrow yet?"

"Soon," he said, chuckling. "Goodnight, Princess Sofia."

He slipped out of the house faster and quieter than I was expecting, and I was left alone in my own living room, stunned, looking at a small pile of, um, was it dust? It smelled like him. I thought I might die.

Chapter 5

We didn't meet again that weekend, because I forgot to get his phone number, and he didn't mysteriously show up at my house again.

I did as much work on the project as I could on my own but it wasn't the same without him there. Especially the kissing part.

By Monday morning I still hadn't heard anything and I was on the verge of anger. I woke up and immediately started practicing the argument we were going to have when I finally saw him again. I want him to like me, but only a monster doesn't do his part of a group project.

I never got a chance to deliver that speech, though, because sitting on the cluttered desk in my room was a 15-page report on Egypt complete with footnotes, suggestions for the presentation, and a handwritten message on a scrap of yellowed paper.

Something came up. Need to leave town. I'm sorry. Thinking about you. -S

Never mind the fact that doing all the work without consulting the group is almost worse than doing nothing, or that a high school student using the phrase "leave town" is super weird, or that the note was written in a pristine hand on what appeared to be papyrus, or that he somehow managed to get in my house and leave again without me noticing. Never mind those things. The important thing to remember is HE'S THINKING ABOUT ME! I MIGHT DIE!

I instantly forgave him for everything else, though I continued to speculate about what "leave town" meant while I got ready for school. I hoped he wasn't in Witness Protection, hiding from the mob. Or that if he was, it was because he witnessed something and not because he was a former mobster. Or if he was a mobster himself, that he wasn't a contract killer. Something reputable like a bookie or a crooked lawyer.

Okay, if he was a contract killer, I could get over that if he only killed people who deserved to be killed. Or if they didn't, if he was repentant and that's why he turned state's evidence. Or if he didn't feel that bad but...

Maybe I sound too forgiving, but let me remind you HE WAS THINKING ABOUT ME. So hike up your judgement pants and walk on out of here, Judgy McJudgerson. I have some remembering to do.

I flopped down on my bed, my legs dangling off the end. I laid there looking at the ceiling but not in focus, thinking about that kiss (two of them, technically!). Yeah, I'd forgive him for being a contract killer of any kind. But I'd make him promise never to go back and do "one more job".

Duncan honked again (or was it the first time? Am I falling apart?) and I reluctantly got up and walked out of room, nearly bumping into the door frame as my brain slowly adjusted back to the real world. This had better not last long or I was going to really hurt myself.

Dunc was waiting in the driveway in his filthy red Jeep.

He leaned out the window flap and tried to be friendly, though something seemed a bit off with him this morning. I probably made him wait too long.

"How'd the project go, Princess?" he asked chipperly as we drove in the direction of Rock Ridge High.

I knew I didn't want to tell Duncan about the kissing part, at least not yet. Probably not the weird note either, but it felt so strange keeping secrets from him. We just didn't keep secrets from each other.

Then again, we came up with that policy before I had anything worth keeping secret from anybody. Maybe it was time to reevaluate the official secret keeping policy.

"It was fine. Seth really knows his Egypt."

"Did you go to his house or did he come up here?"

"Why does it matter?" I asked, way too defensively. I tossed my hair and forced a laugh, which came out even more desperate than I already sounded. Ugh. Maybe that's why we shouldn't keep secrets, because I am *not* good at it.

"I was just wondering," Duncan said, relieving my guilt somewhat. "I bet he lives in a crazy house."

"Oh I'm sure. Not that you're one to talk."

Duncan's house was overflowing with weird treasures from his years of amateur archeology, castings of this and that thing he delicately dug out with a paint brush. Don't even get me started on his porch.

He chuckled. "Fair, fair. But mine are legitimate artifacts. How did your dad like him?"

"A lot, actually. I was surprised."

"Huh." Duncan tightened up again. "Mr. Murdoch doesn't usually like people." There was a mattress ad on the radio and Duncan turned it up, not liking the direction this was taking.

I reached over and turned it back down. Part of my

mind was interested in mattresses all of a sudden, in case Seth ever wants to... but not now, I'm trying to have a fight with Duncan.

"Just say what's on your mind, Duncan. Don't be passive aggressive."

He huffed. "Is he as weird and creepy in person as he is in the cafeteria?"

Now we were getting into it. He didn't like Seth. But Duncan liked everybody. This was getting weird. Why was he being so protective all of a sudden?

"He's not creepy at all. He's soft spoken, but he's really kind, actually," I said.

"You ask him what all the gauzy bandages are about? Was he in some kind of full-body sports injury? Or is he covered in racist tattoos?"

"Of course I didn't ask him that!" My voice dropped down. "You don't just ask people about those things."

"He's wearing them everywhere. It's creepy. Was he in the Yakuza and those are covering up all the tats about crimes he's committed?"

"I think it's probably a cultural thing," I said, getting defensive again. "He wasn't born here, you know."

"I don't like the way he looks at you."

I raised an eyebrow. This just took a turn.

"What? Does he look at me? How does he look at me?"

"Never mind," Duncan self-corrected.

"No, we're talking about this. How does he look at me? When? I want to know!"

"Oh, interesting," he said, turning up the radio again. "That's a good deal for a mattress. I can't afford not to."

"And since when do you care about how--" the ad ended, and I became suddenly aware I was yelling. I tried again, quieter. "Since when do you care how people look at me?"

He turned off the radio and pouted. "I'm sorry I'm being stupid. I've just never felt like this before."

"Felt how, Duncan? Are you hurt? Did something happen on your camping trip? Hey, you haven't told me about the camping trip!" I grabbed his shoulder. "Did somebody wreck your dig site? Did you get some ancient disease that's laid dormant for thousands of years waiting for a host body to inhabit? Did the government mysteriously remove the whole site and pretend nothing ever happened there?"

His face softened, trying to decide if was more fun to stay pouty or describe the soil densities and possible locations of aboriginal dwellings. That's when I knew I had him. Soil densities *always* win with Duncan.

"That would be exciting, if the site just disappeared. But fortunately it was still there and..."

My mind wandered almost immediately to Seth's gaunt cheeks and the way his feet were turned in slightly when he shuffle-walked. And the bandages. I would have to Google around to see what that represents in the Egyptian or Atlantan cultures. But he was just so cute and mysterious and cool and for some reason he was looking at me!

"I found a site that I'm sure has some artifacts. I can't wait to get in there and start digging this summer."

"Uh huh."

"The rocks are arranged perfectly for a summer settlement for a semi-nomadic people. Just like the ones found throughout the Southwest."

"Really cool."

"I'm planning to... we found a grave with a fresh corpse in it, and we dug it up, and it already knew how to play chess."

"Mmm."

"I still beat it because of all the advancements in chess technique since it was alive."

"Oh yeah."

"Just finished him off with a Latvian Gambit and blew his mind."

"Wait..." I narrowed my eyes at him as I returned to focusing on his reality. "Isn't the Latvian Gambit an *opening* move? What are you even talking about, Duncan?"

"Good to know you're at least paying a little bit of attention, Princess."

"Sorry. I'm just tired. I stayed up late last night working on this project."

"With him?"

"No, something came up and he had to leave town. I finished on my own."

"Had to leave town? That's a weird way for a high schooler to talk. Is he in Witness Protection?"

"I know! That's what I was thinking. It would be kind of exciting to live a life on the run from the mob. That could explain a lot about the weird way he acts and dresses."

"Oh yeah. The bandages are to hide his identity. Similar to my Yakuza hypothesis, actually."

"It's not a subtle disguise, but effective."

"Are you going to skip town with him? Bonnie and Clyde? Driving and committing crimes? Is the wedding back on?"

I looked at him seriously. "You know he's not competing with you, right Duncan? You're my best friend and nothing that happens with Seth will change that."

"That's not exactly what I'm worried about. I'd rather we..." he trailed off as we pulled into the school parking lot.

"What? You'd rather what?"

"Never mind. See you at lunch?"

"Definitely. Best friend." I punched him lightly, and he frowned. "Thanks for the ride!"

It was three more days before I saw Seth again. The presentation had gone really well between the work I did and the notes he left. I looked for him every day at lunch but his seat sat empty. Well, I guess he hadn't been at school long enough to have his own seat. That place he sat one time while I stared at him remained hauntingly empty.

Duncan was excited at first to have things back to normal, but when I became insufferably boring to talk to, he said he hoped Seth would return just so I wasn't such a bummer to be around. I had a feeling something was really wrong, and I worried more each day.

At lunch on Thursday, my moping was starting to bore even me, so I tried a new technique I called denial. There was no kiss. How could there be? In fact, there was no Seth at all. That made more sense than a mysterious hot guy showing up, making out with me, writing our geography paper, then leaving town on business. These things don't just happen, especially not to Princess Beige.

I was so busy noticing my own hallucinations as I walked away from the cashier with a full tray of sad-looking food that I didn't even notice the puddle of spilled chocolate milk and the "slippery when wet" sign a lazy custodian had set up instead of mopping up the mess.

I'm normally about as graceful with my body as I am with my words. But that fall was spectacular even for me. My shoes hit the milk and slid forward like I was standing on a treadmill that suddenly turned on turbo, sending my legs out from me so quickly I was horizontal almost instantly. The world slowed down and it felt like I was suspended in the air for at least ten minutes like I was part of a community center magic act.My tray was thus perpendicular to the ground and my tots and salad flew at my face, the lettuce spreading out in a 6-foot radius leaving just a silhouette of an embarrassed head. I stiffened in preparation for the head-cracking collision with the floor, but it never came.

I opened my eyes hoping to figure out why the floor was late for our appointment, and I saw the most beautiful upside-down face.

"You're going to be okay," said the perfect mouth.

"Seth? Why is your face on wrong?"

"What?"

I was so startled by seeing him again I jumped slightly, which was enough to squirm out of his arms. The ground and I finally completed our destiny and connected hard.

I was close enough at that point that it didn't hurt too bad and I popped up as quickly as I could.

"Hey! You can't catch me when I'm falling in the cafeteria because you, my friend, are a hallucination."

He smiled. "Y'know, people usually just say thank you, instead of telling me I don't exist."

"Oh, do you do this a lot?" I tried to sound as dignified as possible while laying in a bed of lettuce and tots. I brushed a slice of mushroom out of my hair.

"It's been known to happen," admitted Seth.

"Well, I'd hate to be the one who was rude. Thank you for saving my life, Mr. Seth." I lowered my voice, as not to alarm him. "Now, I don't know how to break this to you, but you don't exist."

I helped myself up, nearly slipping again on a leaf of romaine, and noticed Seth contorting himself to avoid contact with the chocolate milk. He must be *really* lactose intolerant.

"I'm sorry I had to go," he said, glancing around. "I promise I'll tell you all about it some time. My family is a mess."

I crossed my arms.

"What is it?" he asked.

"I was really looking forward to those tots."

He carefully dabbed at the salad dressing that had splattered on his wrist with a napkin then folded it, and carefully wiped a couple drops off my head.

Behind the kiss, it was the second most romantic thing that'd ever happened to me.

We chatted over the new tots—that he insisted on buying me—until the bell rang and I had to run off. Try as I might to pry it out of him, not even the promise of two and a half tater tots (which he technically owned) could make him tell me a single detail about where he had gone or why.

The longer I attempted to grill Seth, the more it dawned on me how little I knew about him. Where was he from? Atlanta? Egypt, before that? But how long ago? He has this air about him, you know, like he's seen the world and now he's a tiny bit better than you because of it.

His mom passed away when he was young, but what else? Did he have siblings? A cat? An internet famous cat? Where was his dad? How old was he, really? He seemed too smart to be a junior, but there he was, going through junior classes, something nobody would do unless they absolutely had to. I mean, you'd have to be a dangerously unstable person to take Algebra 3-4 if you'd already graduated from high school. Not to mention a major creepster hanging around high schoolers if you were older than 18.

One thing I knew for sure was how he made me feel. Different. Like tingly and allergic, but in a good way. I considered whether or not to tell him he seemed like benevolent ragweed and thought better of it.

Even though he was the one with a family emergency, he seemed much more interested in finding out how I was doing. He asked a ton of questions about the presentation and really seemed to care about the answers. We talked and it was even starting to feel natural. And he laughed. Genuinely. Like he thought I was funny. Go, Beige, go!

As we were leaving the cafeteria, this blond senior named Kate walked up and handed him a slip of paper. Kate was a genuinely nice person, which made it harder to hate her for her perfect looks and natural ability toward every new sport she tried. Jealousy was something I was used to feeling, but I was surprised at how quickly it welled up inside me and over such a small thing. All she had done was talk to my Seth. And he wasn't really mine. She talked to a Seth. That shouldn't make me jealous.

He chuckled and threw the note away but didn't want to talk about its contents.

"Kate just did something brave and misguided, and it doesn't seem right to violate her privacy. But obviously the answer is no."

"The answer to what?"

"It doesn't matter, Princess. But even pouting, your smile is worth a thousand Kates."

"I don't know about that. If infinite monkeys could write Shakespeare, 1,000 Kates could probably manage at least a couple David Mamet plays."

He laughed freely.

"You're the best, Princess."

"I'm okay. You're the best, Seth."

"You should get to class."

"YOU should get to class."

Neither of us moved.

"Okay."

"Okay."

"I'm going now."

"Good idea."

Finally he leaned over and pecked me on the cheek and

then shuffled off, his text books hanging in his limp arm. I floated to English class and nearly bumped into everything on the way.

While I was walking to meet Duncan in the parking lot, Seth shuffled up to me and caught my arm.

"Hi, Princess. Need a ride home?"

"Duncan drives me."

"I really need to talk to you. Can you tell him I'll take you?"

"I don't know," I told him. "My dad doesn't trust me in anybody's car except his own and Duncan's, even though Dunc drives a Jeep, and it's got a really high center of gravity just like he does, so it's probably going to roll over at any moment."

"I'm a great driver. Low center of gravity, not one rollover. And if your dad finds out, you can tell him I've got front and side airbags, the whole nine."

I thought about it some more. How could you not trust those deep dark eye-areas and all that fabric hiding the area around them? He had honest eyeholes, which is definitely an advantage when driving. And his car *was* safer. Dad would be upset if I said no. Okay, I'm making excuses. But I really wanted to ride home with him for a change.

"I guess it can't hurt," I said and texted Duncan not to wait for me.

I was wrong about that part. It hurt Duncan. A lot.

I'd been doing that more and more recently, and he was one guy who would never deserve that. He deserved a better friend. I made a mental note to be a better friend to him or find him a suitable replacement.

But after all that, on the way home, Seth didn't say

much. Or rather, he started to say lots of things, then grunted and stopped himself. Finally, he became frustrated and just shook his head and stared out the windshield, mouth slightly agape, one impossibly thin wrist resting on the steering wheel.

I spent the time admiring just how shiny the inside of his car was. Seth had a white Porsche that looked WAY out of place at a school that heavily favored American-made cars and SUVs. How much camping or fishing gear could you carry in a Porsche? Probably not much at all.

"Just forget it," he said, even though he hadn't said anything yet.

I didn't know what it was and wouldn't have forgotten it anyway, but I figured I had to make him feel comfortable to open up. Plus he had called this meeting, so maybe he thought it was my job to run the agenda. Okay Brain, work your magic--

"I make too much saliva sometimes," I said. And then, mortified, "I'm just going to get out here, don't bother slowing down." I reached for the door handle.

"What?"

He hadn't heard. Maybe I didn't need to throw myself onto the highway.

"Not all the time," I clarified.

"Is it a medical condition?"

"I don't think so. I've checked WebMD. Nothing."

"Is it uncomfortable?"

"I thought for a while it might be rabies but since I was never bitten by anything and this isn't a rabies symptom, I figured no."

"Thanks for sharing, Sofia." He chuckled, but it wasn't mean. He actually did seem grateful.

This was going okay, so I decided to ruin it.

"What did you do to your wrists?" I asked, indicating the bandages peeking out between his sleeves and his stylish driving gloves. Who wears driving gloves? It did look cool, I admitted. But if it weren't for the blasting AC it'd be a million degrees in here.

He pulled on his sleeve and looked away.

"I have this... condition. But it's too embarrassing to talk about. I mean, I don't really have to wear them anymore but... I think they look better than... never mind."

"Do you have rabies?"

"Not as far as I know." He managed between laughs.

"I'd like you to do better than that."

"I'll get tested some time."

"Well, it *does* look good on you. I bet everybody's going to be doing it by the end of the month. People here just copy fashion from the hot guys."

He laughed again. "So I'm hot?"

I didn't even realize I'd said it.

"I should go." I tried to jump out of the moving car again to get away from this whole conversation, but that's when I realized we were in my driveway and he had already shut off the engine. For the best, I guess.

"What is it about you?" He asked, reaching out to touch my chin.

"Not rabies. I can promise you that. But I'm sure if I search hard enough, I'll find out something rare and terrible I suffer from."

He laughed and then leaned in and kissed me lightly. Like the last time, it was wonderful. I had so little experience kissing boys that I didn't know if it was always like this. It was like kissing the desert air; drier than you'd expect, but not in a bad way. His lips were firm but his movements gentle.

We both wiped our mouths on our sleeves, like always. I wondered why they didn't show that part of kissing in the movies. Maybe he was just worried because of my over-saliva problem.

"I'm going to ask you a question and you can't laugh," I said, when he pulled away.

"I can't wait," he said, already looking dangerously close to laughing.

"Stop it! No laughing. Okay, um. Do you want to be my boyfriend?"

His face fell. Definitely not what I'd hoped, but kinda what I expected. I panicked.

"I mean, I understand if you don't, if you'd rather be with Kate, for example. Of course you wouldn't want to be my boyfriend, what a stupid idea. I wouldn't have believed it myself, but then you look at me in this way that really seems like you *do* want to. Not to mention the kissing. That's weird. Most people who like Kate don't kiss me. They usually kiss Kate. What's with that?"

"I don't want to be with Kate."

"Maddy? Emily? Hanna? Emily?"

"Them either."

"I'm sure we can find you a nice girl. What are you into?"

"I'm into you, Sofia. Really. Of course I want to be your boyfriend."

"Super sweet!"

"But..."

"Damnit!" I knew I should have let him finish. "Goodbye forever!"

I opened the door quickly and threw myself out it, expecting a quick and painless death.

I landed on the driveway. Oh right. We're home.

My jeans were dirty and I was still alive, so a double fail.

Seth walked around and crouched next to me, laughing uncontrollably.

"How are you still here? I thought I escaped."

"Oh, Princess Sofia. You're going to be the death of me."

"I was hoping to be the death of me."

He leaned in to kiss me again but I stopped him this time.

"Yeah, you don't get to keep doing that until we figure that other thing out."

He sighed. "That's fair."

"So?"

"I'm sorry, I really am. But I can't be your boyfriend. At least not right now. There's this... I... you need to understand... my condition..."

"There you go again. If you finished half the sentences you started I'd know your whole life story by now. I might even be sick of you talking."

I'm not one for pouting, but it felt so right.

"I need you to promise me you'll stay safe."

"WHAT??"

I was ready to take out my Mace and show him how safe I could stay.

"I need to leave town again," he said. I think he knew this wasn't going well.

"Nope. You don't get to do that either. Not unless you tell me why this time. Or you take me with you."

I stood up and brushed the dust off my pants. He stood too and I stared at him as intensely as I could manage.

"I can't tell you why or where, but you need to believe me. It's for you."

"For me? What are you talking about?"

"Sofia." He was dead serious now. "I need you to promise me you'll stay safe. Don't go places alone. Do what your dad says."

He was the most infuriating boy I'd ever met.

"Do what my dad says? You're insane, Seth. A second ago we were kissing and now you're giving me a news report on car prowlers. I don't know what's going on. I'm leaving."

I started walking down the driveway.

"This is your house."

"I don't care."

He chased me down and walked next to me as I continued walking away, since it was easier than admitting I forgot we were at my house.

"I'm so sorry. I wish I could just tell you everything."

"I'm a genie. Your wish is granted."

"I can't. I--"

"Yes you can! Look, I'll start it for you: 'Sofia, I'm being a cryptic jerk because secretly I'm...'"

He wilted further. "Deep down you must know the end of that sentence already. It's... pretty obvious." He waved his hands over his deep eyes, sallow skin, bandages peeking out underneath his clothes, and stirring smells of the desert.

"What?"

Maybe I did know, but my brain wouldn't let me say it.

He stopped walking.

"Okay, I need to go, Sofia. I'm sorry. I'm going to finish this forever, and then I'll come back, and everything will be fine, and I'll be your boyfriend, and it'll be great."

I turned and looked back at him.

"Maybe I won't wait for you. I have lots of great offers, you know. People pass me secret notes all the time."

He sighed, then walked back to his car.

"Not really though," I yelled after him. "That was a lie

to make you jealous so you'd stay!"

"I'm sorry, Sofia."

He backed up and sped off down the street. Of course, he was right—it was pretty obvious. The weird way he dressed, with all those bandages. His scent. The way he knew everything about Egypt. There was only one logical explanation, and it had been staring me straight in the face: he was too worldly for a small-town girl like me.

His bandages were probably a new Parisian trend that I'd never catch on to. By "condition" he probably meant that he was just so cool doctors are studying him.

I bet his dusty desert cologne was made in small batches by an obscure designer that you could only buy in places I'd never visit. Plain and simple, he was a globe trotting playboy hipster and way out of my league.

He was the one who started this whole thing, which was pretty rude! I always knew he was unobtainable, that's why I just wanted to stare at him over my text book. He's the one that escalated this from staring all the way to kissing. He kissed *me*! I didn't kiss *him*. If he's embarrassed to be kissing a girl who doesn't wear cool bandages and dusty perfumes and know about other countries, that's his problem. He should stop kissing that girl. I'm beige. Either that's good enough for him or it's not.

I'd been so swept up in feeling cool that I forgot about the people who cared about me. And now I couldn't talk to Duncan—he would say he told me so. I couldn't talk to my dad—he would just suggest Mace. I couldn't talk to Bastian—he's a cat and cats don't talk.

I stormed into the house.

"Hi, Princess! Sorry, I burned the--"

I slammed the door to my bedroom. I was alone.

Chapter 6

Saturday morning I awoke as if coming back from the dead. I bolted upright, unable to remember the dream that frightened me so much.

I looked around the room, and I could see where Seth had been because he'd tracked that weird grey dust all over. It was going to be near impossible to clean up all those particles, but even that seemed easier than scrubbing him out of my life.

I hadn't thought much about the dust he left behind before now, but I started to imagine possibilities.

Gardener? Nah, wrong kind of dirt.

He's always going through people's attics and getting covered in their dust? Explains his vintage jewelry. Maybe he even owns his own boutique. I labeled that one as plausible.

Oh, maybe he's an amateur archaeologist, like Duncan. Dunc was always showing up covered in powdery dust. I would have been excited to learn that my best friend and not-quite-boyfriend had something in common, but since my not-boyfriend had just not-broken up with me, it would actually be more sad than anything else.

Or maybe he's an astronaut, and this is moon dust. He's not just more worldly than me, he's more galactic. "There's this restaurant on Mercury where only the coolest kids go. I'm going to take my girlfriend Space Katie there tomorrow, and we're going to space make out because she's done that before."

"SHUT UP IMAGINARY ASTRONAUT SETH I HATE YOU," is a thing I shouted alone in my room.

Not proud of it.

It's all for the best. How could an intergalactic hipster ever be happy with a meh-looking, funny-ish girl suffering from a saliva imbalance? I was fooling myself. Our relationship was only worth three, three and a half kisses, tops. I'm lucky it lasted as long as it did.

Dad must've known something was up because he arranged my fried eggs and bacon into a smirking face with one eye burnt shut. Maybe it was winking?

"It was supposed to be happy," he said, when I stumbled into the kitchen and saw the plate. "Do you want some toast eyebrows or are you already sufficiently cheered up?"

The knob on our toaster didn't even go below 5. I passed.

"You're not even going to ask me what's wrong?" I picked up a piece of blackened bacon and pushed around the winking eye suspiciously.

"What's the point? The odds of you wanting to tell me are very low. And then the odds that I'd understand anyway, even lower. Not to mention the odds that I'd give good advice, you'd take it, and it'd actually help?" He whistled. "I'd say no better than 600k to one."

"Better than lightning," I offered. "And that happens to people all the time."

He brightened. "You remembered my lightning facts!"

"Sure," I said. "A weatherman's daughter needs to know a few things. You'd be surprised how often that comes in handy, actually."

"Yeah?"

"Usually to scare away somebody who thought I'd be fun to talk to."

"Still counts," he said, and chuckled.

I tried to saw my egg-eye in half with the bacon, but it broke.

"Bottom line is, most problems you can't talk about," Dad said, gesturing with his own burnt bacon-mouth professorially. "Some go away on their own, some don't. But you usually don't get anywhere talking about 'em. But almost all of them, you can eat about."

"I didn't say I had a problem."

"And I didn't ask. If it's small, it'll seem better after breakfast. If it's big, at least you had one good meal before the state drags you away and executes you."

"Whoa, I definitely didn't commit any capital crimes, Dad," I said, my mouth full of yolk/retina.

"Hey, save it for the judge, jailbird. I'm just the cook."

"Prison food might be an improvement, actually. I hear they don't burn the eggs there."

"And that's why I always say prison is dangerous."

"That's the reason you think prison is dangerous?"

He took my ribbing in stride, picking up his mug of extra-dark roast coffee and raising it in my direction as he leaned against the counter. The only sounds were me chewing.

"I think I will take those toast eyebrows after all," I said. Eating about this problem was actually helping.

He dropped them on the plate, and I crunched into the

first one.

"Seth left town because he's too cool for me."

"I thought I said I didn't want to hear your problems."

"Also, we kissed a few times."

"Oh fun. How'd that go?" He wasn't as surprised as I'd expected.

"Good, I think."

"Well, alright then."

"But I feel stupid now," I said. "For thinking it was something more. And I miss him. And I feel stupid for missing him."

"Sounds about right," he said.

"Is that all you got?" I said in mock anger. "I opened up to you!"

He shrugged. "If you feel stupid, it usually means you've learned something and you're less stupid now. So that's a win. And if you've learned that some boys are dicks, that's another win. Some are nice but do dickish things because they don't know any better. And some do nice things but are kinda dicks about it."

"Which one is he?"

"If he comes back, you can ask him. Then you can Mace him to make sure he learned something, too."

"Didn't you say 'Mace first, ask questions later'?"

"That *does* sound like me. I guess it depends on how much sputtering you want him to do when he answers the question."

I sighed. "But what if he doesn't come back?"

"You still know more about yourself than you used to, Princess. You've learned what you need in a relationship to be happy, and that's a valuable lesson. The next time a mysterious guy wants to come over and study, you can tell him how you need to be treated. And if he doesn't, Mace the crap out of him and ask questions later. Or don't even ask the questions."

"Thanks, Dad."

"Don't Mace him so much that you have to go to jail, though. I've just heard some terrible news about the food safety there."

"I don't know if that makes me feel better or way worse," I said, smiling.

"Hey, I'm just the cook," he said, and raised his mug to me again. "I've got to give a weather report from the parking lot of a car dealership for some reason. Have a good day, Princess."

As I showered and got dressed, I went over Dad's advice in my head. Even though it didn't make me feel any better, what he said had made a lot of sense. And he hadn't panicked, which put everything in perspective. Maybe I'll take more problems to him and eat about them.

Duncan met me in the driveway. When I had texted him to see if he wanted to hang out, it had taken him 10 minutes to write back. It was the longest he'd ever taken by 9 and a half minutes. When he saw me, it took about 10 minutes for him to smile, too.

"I'm sorry, Duncan," I said, getting in the passenger seat of his Jeep. "I know you're mad. I thought maybe we can just go somewhere to talk."

"Anywhere in particular?"

"Anywhere sounds great."

We pulled up in front of The Desert King's Mini-Golf Adventure, and I frowned at him.

"You must be really pissed," I said.

Duncan gave an innocent shrug as if he'd forgotten how much I hated mini-golf. The most, that's how much I hated it.

"You said anywhere, Princess," he said as he dismounted from the Jeep. The heat of the parking lot would have been enough to knock me over if I hadn't been so busy worrying about golfing.

Miniature golf is the stupidest in a long line of stupid pastimes forced on uncoordinated children by their optimistic parents hoping to find a family activity for their kids to become decent at. See also: ice skating, laser tag, and above all, bowling.

This particular uncoordinated child attended many years of birthday parties at the mini-golf course. And yes, many of those birthdays had been with Duncan. And yes, there was always a generous helping of mulligans and pity-putts before the greatest indignity, kicking the ball into the hole.

Mini-golf is what the Spanish Inquisition developed when people got too used to the rack.

"Two, please," Duncan said to the ball jockey through the metal bars of his snack shack. "The lady will be paying."

"Jeez, Dunc. Did I insult your mom too?" I asked. "Even the inquisitors didn't make their victims pay for the whips."

"Come now, Princess. You don't want to keep the Desert King waiting."

I slid cash under the bars and the kid almost looked up, but not quite.

The Desert King was a Rock Ridge legend. He was the biggest celebrity in town, despite being completely fictional and completely ridiculous. Nobody remembered who had created him in the first place, which is what made him such a good endorser. He hocked anything and everything and it cost nothing.

The King would endorse his favorite shake, his favorite oil change, and his favorite decaying mini golf course.

You couldn't drive a block without seeing some version of that face: dark, powerful eyes with a hint of black eyeliner and a pointy chin with gold braided into his black goatee. He usually wore an ornate and top-heavy gold headdress with a serpent sticking out, though his hat was frequently changed to reflect the business he was supporting. He looked silly normally, but much sillier with a "Rock Ridge Tire Co" baseball cap on.

The whole city's obsession with Ancient Egypt was odd, since we'd never been ruled by a pharaoh and, you know, weren't in Egypt. But when your town is as boring as Rock Ridge (heck, the name is basically synonymous with "Well, I'll sit here for a bit but I won't stay"), you have to do something. Since Baker already had the world's largest thermometer, we decided to go for largest inexplicable cultural appropriation.

After the second hole, Duncan was one under par and I had a perfect score: 12. That's a pair of six-and-outs, meaning I still hadn't actually succeeded in putting the ball in the hole on purpose. There should be a rule where you can just 108-and-out the whole course and go home.

I lost my temper almost immediately on hole #1 when my ball bounced off a concrete rattlesnake and rolled back towards the starting rubber mat and past it, meaning each stroke was bringing me further from my actual goal. The only thing worse than miniature golf is miniature golf that also feels like a metaphor for your life.

My mood wasn't improved by the weather; we were both sweating profusely in the 103 degree sun, and I'd re-applied sunscreen twice since arriving. No wonder we were the only people dumb enough to be playing tiny fake golf right now.

"You've had your fun. I'm sorry I didn't pay much attention to you after I met Seth."

Duncan cringed when I said the name and pounded the

ball into the parking lot. His shoulders slumped.

"Even Tiger Woods misses sometimes," I offered. "I'm sure he's hit a parking lot or two."

"Sof, you really don't get this?" he asked, frustrated. "You don't get why I might be upset? Why even if it's not fair, I hate the thought of you hanging out with him?"

I looked at Duncan. I mean, I really looked at him. He was about to cry on a mini-golf course, something I'd done more than once. And right in front of the Desert King's favorite sarcophagus.

"We've been together for long enough, Sofia. You must know how I feel. About you. About us. How *this* makes me feel." He gestured with one massive arm at the space between us. I could see the veins on his forearm popping out, and suddenly, I got it. It was so obvious. How could I have spent so much time with him and not know? I'm an idiot.

"Oh, Duncan, I am so sorry. This must have been so hard for you."

He sniffed and leaned on his putter. "Thank you. It *has* been hard."

"I should have realized earlier. I just thought the steroids were a harmless phase and they wouldn't affect you this way. I was blind," I said.

He just looked at me. It must have felt good to have me know.

"I mean all these mood swings you've had to deal with, then Seth comes along and he's so effortlessly cool and skinny—that must have brought up all the body issues that made you feel like you needed to change the way you look," I said. "But you're my best friend, even if you can't fit in skinny jeans. Because I really value our friendship." I gave him a reassuring pat on the shoulder.

"Sofia," he said, looking sad and befuddled, probably at the fact that it took me so long to notice. The hormones were really doing a number on him. "Can't you see that I'm in love with--"

Before he could finish his sentence, a golf club clocked him in the back of the head, and he went down like a sack of lumpy teddy bears.

I turned, with no way to comprehend what was happening.

"Hey, asshole, you could've killed him!"

Two men, one little and one big, stood on the third green, the little one holding a golf club and smacking it into his palm. "Killed? Nah. You need way more force than that."

The little one had a goatee, and the big one had a couple chins but no hair on any of them and a matching shaven white head. They were both dressed in loose white linen shirts and pants. The big one reached over and caught the windmill from hole #7, tearing off one of the blades and casually wielding it in my direction.

"Hello, Princess," he said, making it sound like a threat.

They took a step closer to me.

"Uh, do I know you?" I dropped my golf club. As the panic rose, my mouth filled and words tumbled out. "I don't recognize you. And the way you're dressed, I don't think we go to the same school or anything." I fumbled in my back pocket. "I'm pretty sure I'd recognize you. I'm great with faces. I could describe every face from my 3rd grade class. Want to hear?"

"I'm Eli," said the little one. He pointed up at his multi-chinned companion. "This is Bunny."

"'Allo," said Bunny amicably.

"Your friend will probably be okay," said Eli. "Unfortunately, you have a different destiny. The Priest is going to--"

I whipped out my canister of Mace and started pulling

the trigger before I got it fully aimed. Even still, Dad would have been proud.

The spray painted an arc in the sky, eventually making contact with Eli's face. I aimed for the eyes, of course, but even though he was smaller than Bunny, he still towered over me so most of it went up his nose. He fell to the ground, coughing and sputtering.

I turned toward Bunny and kept spraying, screaming the whole time. His reaction time was better than his friend's, though, so he spun the windmill blade at the same time and it connected with my hand, knocking my only weapon to the ground and bruising my knuckles.

Bunny wagged his mill blade at me. "You shouldn't have done that. Now Bunny is mad."

He stepped closer, and I couldn't move. Body, this is Brain. Get the hell out of here. Now. Go. Go. Go. Nothing. Body wasn't answering her phone.

As Bunny reached out to grab me, something happened that surprised me more than being attacked on a putt-putt course by somebody named Bunny: the big man was swarmed by cats. Like, a *lot* of cats.

Thousands of stray cats poured onto the course like a herd of migrating buffalo. They lept with claws extended onto Bunny's overflowing body. He screamed in a register that closely resembled mine, and tried to tear the cats off his chest and legs. Each one he threw off pulled pieces of his clothes, hair, or flesh in their tiny, underfed claws, and then the empty space was instantly replaced by three more cats.

Bunny gave up the individual approach and tried shaking violently like a wet dog, which temporarily threw off enough cats that he could stagger back from the herd. He grabbed Eli by the scruff of his collar, tossed him over his shoulders like a sack of potatoes, and made a hasty retreat.

Bunny moved quicker than I'd have expected for such a big man, especially one carrying another big man and suffering from hundreds of scratches. A couple cats gave chase, but most of them formed a protective circle around me and sat back, licking their claws clean.

I numbly moved toward Duncan to check on him, but in the sea of cats I didn't notice the small concrete pyramids blocking the 7th hole. I rolled my ankle and toppled over, but just before I hit the ground a soft, dry hand caught me.

"You survived the fight and then tried to die in the aftermath? You're something else."

My eyes were still closed, preparing for impact with the green turf, but this time I didn't need to see him to know who he was.

"Thanks, Seth," I whispered hoarsely, "but these cats and I were doing just fine without you."

"I know," he said. "I just thought you'd want some help with cleanup."

"Thanks? But I've got it handled. I just hope that Bunny character comes back so I can finish macing him to death," I said more bravely than I felt.

"Burying a body is harder than you think," Seth said almost wistfully.

"Okay, this game isn't fun anymore. You sound like an actual hardened killer, instead of just a dick." I opened my eyes and stared up into his. I tried to stay mad but I just couldn't when I saw his perfect, shrouded face. "Ugh, why are you so handsome?"

He smiled. "I'm handsome?"

"Now isn't the time. Put me down, Captain Abandoner. Let's call Animal Control about these cats."

When I looked around, though, there wasn't a single cat to be found.

"Did I hallucinate them? Was that the Mace? Did I inhale some myself?"

"You probably did, which is why your eyes are watering, but the cats were real. They saved you and Duncan before I could get here to protect you."

"Oh God, Duncan! Is he dead?"

"He'll be alright," said Seth. "They would have made sure not to kill him. They wouldn't want to draw any attention from local authorities."

"You sound like you're practically friends with them."

"Quite the opposite. But they've been after me for a long time."

"Oh, Jesus. I knew it. You're in Witness Protection because you're a hired killer, and I didn't have time to decide if I was okay with that! Please tell me you only kill people who deserve it, that at least will make it a little easier."

"What are you talking about, Sofia?"

"What are you talking about?"

"They're not mobsters, you weirdo. They're grave robbers."

"Oh good. Thanks for clearing everything up. I'm the weirdo for thinking they were mobsters, but grave robbers makes all the sense in the world. Super thanks."

I wanted to scream at him. Once, just once, I wanted something he said not to be the weirdest thing I'd ever heard. I gave him one final chance.

"Fine, I'll bite. Whose grave were they trying to rob? Because I'm pretty sure the one on hole #14 isn't real."

He whispered his answer. "They're after my grave."

"I give up."

I wriggled out of his hands and landed on my butt. He reached for my arm but I pushed him away and got up, brushing off my pants. "Duncan and I are leaving now. We have a police report to file. And PS: it is clearly you who is the weirdo here." Boom. That'll teach him.

Maybe "grave" was a cool name hipsters call their apartments, and maybe he has some amazing vintage jewelry they could be trying to rob, but I just didn't need any of this in my life. Dad was right, even when he does nice things, Seth does them in a dickish way.

I bent down over Duncan. He was just starting to regain consciousness.

"Dunc, we need to get you to a hospital."

"Oh no you don't," he slurred. "Trying to get out of 16 holes of mini-golf just because I got hit in the head? You probably planned this."

"Duncan," I said, "You were unconscious for three minutes. That's not supposed to happen."

"Man, you hate this game more than I thought if you paid somebody to assault me."

He blinked hard as he saw Seth standing over us.

"Okay, the mummy from hole #7 is looking at me. Maybe I do have a concussion?"

Seth looked like he was about to say something but I stopped him.

"I'm pretty mad at Seth right now too, but you don't need to make fun of the way he dresses. I'll finish this game if you promise I can take you to the hospital immediately after."

"Deal."

It shouldn't have been hard to beat a concussed Duncan, but the game took three hours, and he still managed to win 54 to 106. I hate mini golf.

Chapter 7

After Duncan got a clean bill of health from the hospital, Seth drove us both back home. I had to squish into the tiny back seat of his Porsche to make room for Duncan, who had a bandage around his head and was a bit loopy from the pain killer they gave him. In his state, he thought that his bandage resembled Seth's hipster head wrapping and that the similarity was the best joke he'd ever heard. He kept touching Seth's and his own head at the same time and giggling.

"We're twins, Seth. You were so cool; well, I can be cool too."

Seth didn't seem to appreciate the joke, but he focused on the road. I thought he took it better than most hipsters would if you made fun of their carefully selected outfits.

I was just glad to be done with the whole thing. When I got home I flopped down in bed and told Bastian that some cats saved my life while he sat around doing nothing, but he didn't seem impressed.

I had homework and sleep to catch up on but my brain

just wouldn't shut off. There was something about the day that still felt a bit strange. Was it the army of cats that showed up to save my life and then evaporated? No, that checked out. The grave robbers who showed up, domed Duncan, and called me Princess like they knew me? The fact that as I got older I somehow got even worse at miniature golf while Duncan seemed to improve even while suffering from a traumatic brain injury? No, there was something deeper tying it all together, and Seth was at the center of it.

We couldn't really talk while Duncan was there, so we'd agreed to meet the next day, but I couldn't stop thinking— was he really a normal if above-averagely-hot teenage boy after all?

I opened my laptop and stared at the screen. A funny thing happened. I didn't immediately go to Ancestry.com. I didn't even want to. I couldn't quite make sense of what I'd gotten caught up in, and the only way I was going to straighten any of it out was to Google the shit out of it.

I started tentatively with "hipsters", skimming the results carefully. Soon my fingers were flying over the keys, and I had 30 tabs open with answers to different questions. I clicked around, closing the useless ones, which was most of them. Lots of beard oil and music blogs. Something about cold brew coffee and terroir. Some very well-dressed toddlers. I tried everything I could think of to locate Seth's distinct fashion sense. There were hoodies aplenty but none quite like his. Was he that cutting edge?

The bandaged look seemed to be completely unique to him, which could just mean that he wasn't a poser, but an actual trend setter. I let that sink in. A guy who can single handedly make body wrapping happen was way out of my league.

Still, my first thought could have been right: he could have a horrible disease. I spent a disgusting 5 minutes on WebMD looking for something that might necessitate so many bandages. I saw things I could not unsee, but nothing that matched my Seth.

I closed everything and started over.

Egypt generated lots of news: politics, riots, and the economy. Intermixed were pages and pages about ancient times. Nothing jumped out at me about boyfriends.

As I typed *grave robbers*, my breathing got heavy. I was close to something, something big. And I wasn't sure if I even wanted to know what.

First thing I learned was that grave robbers weren't really a thing anymore, which made their sudden appearance even more surprising. There were instances of pilfering from the dead, sure, but they were mostly confined to rural areas and 1920's era graves that might hold fancier-than-expected jewelry. There were also meth heads who stole copper grave markers to sell as scrap metal, though I have no idea how they explained themselves when they showed up to a metal recycler carrying a plaque that said "Rest in Peace, Dave".

Nothing I could find suggested that grave robbers were burly, traveled in packs, or attacked teenagers with putters. Creepy thieves with no respect for the deceased, yes. Thugs, no.

A dozen clicks into my grave robber search, I saw something that made my heart drop into my stomach.

It was a black and white photo surrounded by a yellowed border and dotted with imperfections as a result of being scanned into a database at the Library of Congress. It showed an ancient Egyptian tomb shortly after it was discovered, and there were signs that the tomb had been pillaged by grave robbers. The attached article was about the detrimental effects of grave crimes on archaeological efforts—Duncan would have been furious—but something in the background caught my eye: a painted sarcophagus, presumably resembling the man buried inside. I gasped. The mummy in the painting was wearing the same hoodie Seth that always wore.

Well, on the painted mummy it looked more like a short ceremonial robe, but it was the same. It had the same markings, which I always assumed was the logo for an indie punk band I hadn't heard about yet. And it had the same amber-studded drawstrings. It was Seth's hoodie.

My hands shaking, I went back to the search bar. My next searches were slow, one letter at a time, like my hands didn't want to be any part of what my brain suddenly knew.

Mummy
Are mummies real
Hipster mummy
Sexy mummy
Can mummies have sex?

Wait, no. I definitely didn't do that last one. Close window. Clear history. Start over.

Watch yourself, Fingers. We need to present a unified front here.

There were articles, links to various horror movies, and images: images of horrible, gaunt, partially decomposed corpses. Mixed in were adorable cartoon depictions of staggering, toilet-paper-wrapped monsters. And especially with "sexy mummy", Halloween costumes I wouldn't be caught dead in.

My dad yelled up at me, and I quickly minimized my browser like a criminal caught in the act.

"The guy you kissed is at the door. I told you that these things work themselves out!"

Mortified at the thought of Seth hearing this, not to

mention my dad saying it out loud, I rushed downstairs. I lightly punched Dad on the shoulder as I pushed by him then stepped out the door past a surprised Seth.

"Let's go for a walk. Somewhere my dad isn't."

"Okay," he said, chuckling. "So you told him?"

"I'm not as withholding of information as you are."

He sighed. "I deserve that."

We headed down the block. The sun was just setting, and the air was starting to get that chill of a desert night. It was clear out, but the sliver of moon didn't add much light. The stucco walls prevented us from seeing into the neighbors' houses, but there were a few lights on and some flickering TVs. A street light every other block would light up our way for 10 feet, then we'd slowly be engulfed in darkness again. I was glad for the darkness because I was pretty sure I was already blushing, and I didn't want Seth to know.

"You showed up at a mini golf course too late to save me from anachronistic criminals after turning down my generous offer of boyfriend status and disappearing, so you definitely have to start this one," I said.

"I didn't know that was the rule."

I shook my head. "You seem so smart, and yet the basic rules of etiquette elude you."

"Okay, about the grave robbers. It's just that um, they're here because... argh." Instead of talking he just scratched at his face.

We approached a small park I used to play in as a kid.

"Come on, I want to swing."

Without the light we had to walk carefully over the bark around the slides, eventually settling into the two adjacent swings. I pushed myself lazily with my feet. He stayed eerily still.

"You're doing that thing again, where you're not getting past the first two words of your sentences," I pointed out.

"I know. This sentence is particularly hard. You have no idea."

"That's just it. I have no idea. A fact that you could remedy by, I don't know, telling me the truth for once."

"I'm doing my best." His right arm wrapped around his body to scratch his left elbow, and he looked down at his feet. "You have to know by now that there's something different about me, right?"

"That's pretty damn obvious," I said. "For one, you don't know how to talk to other human beings. For another, your skin seems to itch all the time. Have you heard of lotion?"

"That's not it. Something is really different. And I don't do lotion."

"Okay, oil then."

"More my speed but you're stalling."

"I'm stalling? You're the one who's supposed to tell me what the hell you are."

"You know what I am."

"No, I don't. I'm dying to find out though."

"Don't say it that way."

"How should I say it?"

"Just say it."

"Why is this on me again, Seth? This is definitely your turn but you keep passing."

"It's better if you say it. It's right there on the tip of your tongue. Just say it."

"You're a…"

"Say it."

"A… a…" Finally I just blurted it out. He'll have to deal with it. "A hipster."

"What?" He burst out laughing. "I'm a hipster?"

"Well sure, the skinny jeans, the bandages, the gaunt look, the perfect hoodie. That chic, dusty cologne you wear. You probably have great taste in music and coffee."

"You're amazing."

"What's that supposed to mean?"

"Sofia, that's not at all what I'm talking about. Can't you see what I am?"

Now I was confused. "Well you're definitely not a jock. Kinda goth in your demeanor, but you wear really light colors."

"No. But it's more than just what clique I belong to. Look at me. I'm covered in bandages, afraid of moisture, smell like sand, grave robbers started showing up in your life right after I did..."

"You're in the mob."

"No."

"You're on drugs! Oh God, I knew it."

"I'm not on drugs. Jesus, Sofia. I'm a mummy. I'm clearly a mummy. ... How can you not see that?"

I felt his words in my chest. He's a mummy. A walking, talking reanimated corpse Had I known all along? No, probably not. That would be a ridiculous conclusion for me to have come to. This one isn't on me.

But the facts were staring at me from his hollow eye sockets: the logo on his hoodie was the same as the mummy in the picture.

"You're a mummy."

"I'm a mummy."

"But mummies are dead. And you're walking around kissing people."

"In many cases, they are dead. But a lot of us are cursed to walk the earth. Kind of... undead. And I've only kissed the one person."

"Like vampires?"

"No, vampires aren't real."

"But if you're real, there must be loads of other magical creatures that are real too. Werewolves?"

"Nope. Just mummies."

"You've only kissed me? Wait, how about witches? Are they real?"

"Pretty much just mummies. And yes, you're the only person I've kissed."

"Alright Mr. Smartypants, then who made the mummies?" I asked, one eyebrow raised.

"Fine," he said sighing. "There are some magical priests and stuff like that. But really it's just mummies and other creatures that are directly related to mummies."

"So there are wizards."

"Not exactly. Mummies, Priests, that's it."

"What about--"

He cut me off. "Sofia. It's just mummies. And maybe Sasquatch. We're not sure."

"Really?"

"I'm kidding. It's just mummies!"

"How can you joke about this?"

"Uh, I've had more time to process this than you have, obviously. Speaking of which, you're much calmer about this than I expected. I just told you I'm an undead monster and all you can ask about is if vampires are real too."

"I'm just trying to get a grasp on the world I live in now. Are poltergeists real?"

"Just mummies. Listen, you're not grossed out by me? You're not terrified? You kissed a mummy. Twice."

"Technically a mummy kissed me." I said. "I think that makes all the difference. And it was three times."

"Fine, but... you're not running away." It was a state-ment, not a question.

"I can't run away from you, Seth. I don't know what it is or why it is, but it is. There's something about you."

He shook his head. "You're drawn to the danger."

"It's not that at all. I don't even like rollercoasters be-cause they seem too dangerous. I'm drawn to you because you're hot. And because you really seem to care about what happens to me. You were there when I got attacked today, you caught me when I tripped that one time. And the geog-raphy presentation. You're there for me, even when I think you've gone forever."

He cocked his head and looked at me with those deep, grey eyeholes that I was powerless against.

"You're right about that. I've always been there for you, and I always will be."

He leaned in to kiss me. I pulled back.

"Wait, wait. So what about trolls? Do trolls exist?"

"Just mummies. Now shut up and let me kiss you."

"What about--"

And then he kissed me. Four times now.

It was weird but I liked it. It was like being in an attic—dusty, but electric with possibility. He wiped his mouth with his sleeve, and I didn't copy him. I didn't need to.

A young couple with a baby stroller walked by talking quietly. Even in the dim light, we were probably kissing too much for a playground. I just couldn't help myself. The whole world melted away when I was with him.

Kissing him had always been new and exciting, but it was drier than I expected, and his lips weren't exactly in pristine condition, with the lower one hanging slight-ly lower than one would hope. At first I had chalked it up to my inexperience at kissing and his refusal to use Chapstick, but now I knew it was something different. He was a 5,000-year-old reanimated corpse. No. He was MY 5,000-year-old reanimated corpse.

We stood up and started walking toward my house. He took my hand gingerly.

"One of the grave robbers said something that really bothered me," I said casually.

"You're going to need to let them go, Sofia."

"In my defense, somebody tried to kill me today. The least I can do is think about it for a second."

"I guess you're right."

"He said something about knowing my fate. I don't remember exactly. But really the whole time they were attacking us, they seemed to know me. Which is crazy, because I know zero grave robbers in real life."

He was silent for a minute.

"Sofia, there's a lot more to this than I've told you."

"That's the least surprising thing I've heard all day, including my dad telling me it would be hot out. I'm shocked—SHOCKED—to learn you've been withholding information from me."

"It may feel like I've involved you in something terrible. But really, you've always been involved," he said. "This is harder to say than the mummy thing, which was pretty hard, but I was actually sent to protect you, Sofia. We didn't meet by chance."

"It's fun how you manage to make things both vague and extremely creepy at the same time."

"I'm trying, Princess. I really am. And the sarcasm, while entertaining, isn't helping me get through this."

"I'm not sure it's my job to make this easier on you." I smiled and he feebly squeezed my hand. "But that's another thing. They called me Princess too, the Grave Robbers. What's that about?"

"I'll tell you the whole story some time."

"Are they going to come after me again?"

"Yes."

"Promise me you won't leave me this time?"

"I'll never you leave you again, Sofia. No matter what."

I lightly stroked the palm of his hand, careful not to damage the fragile bone remnants.

"Centaurs. Half real?"

A sigh. "Just. Mummies."

Chapter 8

I brushed the sand from my face before I opened the front door so it wouldn't be completely obvious I'd been making out with dusty remains of a mummified teenager.

My dad was waiting for me in the living room, frowning.

"Did you have a nice time?"

"Yes, thank you. I think I've worked out that he was a nice boy who sometimes did dickish things."

"That's good, Sofia. I think it's time we had a chat. Why don't you sit down?"

Suddenly I noticed it—the smell of Dutch apple crisp overbaking in the oven. I froze.

One of my dad's life philosophies was that hard conversations were easier over pie. I still remember the ashen remains of a lemon meringue he made when mom left. Maybe the pie helped the sting of her leaving, but more likely, her leaving ruined pie for me forever.

"I'm definitely not in the mood for a pie talk tonight, Dad."

"I'm sorry, Princess. I've put this off for long enough

already. Maybe too long. Please sit."

I couldn't figure out a way around it so I gritted my teeth, sat down at the dining room table, and prepared myself for Pie Talk: The Sex Talk edition. I thought for sure I'd dodged that bullet at this point, but maybe he thought it was better late than never. I was not looking forward to the metaphors he used to describe sex. My money was on bowling, since that was the only sport he really understood well. It was probably too much to ask, but I hoped he'd leave my gutters out of the analogy.

He might even try darts, which would be even worse.

"Sofia," he started. He was more nervous than I expected. "When you ran off with Seth, you left your computer open."

Oh no! I was still dealing with Seth's revelation about his mummyhood myself; I definitely wasn't ready to explain it to dad. Please, make this a sex talk! Even one about darts and gutters!

"I didn't mean to snoop! I really didn't. I just happened to see Ancestry.com open, and I assumed it was about your research project so I read closer."

"Wait, what?"

"I want you to know it's okay to talk to me about your mom."

"This isn't about sex or mummies?"

"Oh God no. Do you need the sex talk too? Because when you're bowling--"

"No!"

"Whew. As far as mummies go, there's no reason for you still to be scared of them because they're not real."

"That's how I feel, too."

Now we were both confused. He got up to take the pie out of the oven.

"Apple crisp? It's a very dark golden brown."

"Thanks." It actually wasn't too bad for dad's cooking.

He cut a generous slice for each of us and set them on the table, then looked at me seriously.

"How long have you been researching your mom's family?"

I was so relieved not to be talking about mummies or sex or sexy mummies or sex with mummies that I couldn't lie. Or maybe he was right. The pie softens you.

"This whole time. I mean, right after she left."

He put his hand on mine.

"I know this is hard for you, Sofia. But you need to move on."

"I know. I guess I just thought... I don't know, I thought that if I knew everything about her family... maybe I'd understand why she left." I finished the sentence quietly. Even with the pie, that was a hard thing to say out loud.

"I've thought the same thing too. But it won't bring her back."

"I still miss her."

"Me too. Every day."

I'd always thought of my mom leaving as mostly something she did to me. Now I felt guilty for not realizing how much harder it must have been for him. Maybe it was because he was so strong for me.

"When did you know you were in love with her?"

"Not right away," he said with his mouth full of pie. "You might be too young to understand this, but the rush you feel, the first time you think you're in love, that's only the beginning. Love has all these other parts, and they're even bigger and come much later. Like picking up a tough spare in a tournament setting."

"Geez, Dad."

"Sorry, would you prefer I use darts?"

"NO."

"We're running out of games I understand."

"Did she ever give you any sign that she was going to leave?"

"Not exactly. But there was something about her, something about how she glanced over her shoulder at night, she never seemed quite comfortable. There was a restlessness to her, like her past might start chasing her at any moment. I knew she had a dark history she didn't like to talk about."

This was news. It was also vague, as if my dad and Seth went to the same school of conversation.

"Do you know what it was?"

"Like I said, she didn't like to talk about it. But there's something you need to understand about your mom: she, I mean you too, you both come from a long line of, well you probably know from your research."

"Only children?"

He laughed. "Technically true, but there's more than that. Hasn't your research turned it up yet?"

"No?" I had no idea what he was talking about now. My research into my mom's family had turned up a whole lot of nothing. They married young, had only one daughter, and they liked to live in hot places. Those were the only patterns I had found, and those didn't make any sense.

"Well, maybe it's not true then. Supposedly, your mom's family descends from Egyptian royalty. That's why we always called you Princess."

Normally that would just be a silly family legend, but given what I'd been learning recently with Seth and the attacks, I assumed this was more important than Dad made it sound.

"Do you know for sure?"

"Nope. But your mom believed it. She had several pieces of jewelry passed down from her mom's family. Really old stuff. We had them checked out by a couple Egyptologists, and they all were genuine. That was when she started seeming distant, like something was catching up with her. She didn't say it, exactly, but I knew. Her past called to her, like a ringing 10 pin."

It still didn't make sense. Why would realizing she was from royal blood change her like that? It was ancient history.

"Can I see the jewelry?"

"I wish I could give them to you. They're your birthright. But your mom took them when she left. She left everything else; that's why I knew she wasn't ever coming back."

We sat in silence for a few minutes. I pushed the pie around with my fork, knowing even Dutch apple couldn't soften this one. It was going to take a lot of processing. I couldn't help feeling betrayed, but now I wasn't mad. I was confused. I was missing critical information, as usual.

Between this and Seth I'd already gotten enough revelations in one afternoon to last a lifetime. And I still didn't understand. Somehow the two were related and that made me nervous.

"There won't ever be a good answer for this, sweetie, but you have to know that your mom really wanted what's best for you. If she left, she didn't think she had a choice. And if she didn't say where she was going, it's because she didn't think it was safe to follow her. She must have taken the jewels because they were too dangerous for you to keep."

"Dangerous? How?"

"I don't know, Princess."

And that's when I remembered the grave robbers.

They knew something about my fate that I didn't. Were they looking for mom's jewels? Or were they after Seth? Ugh, thinking of him in a grave was still hard for me, even though I know he survived.

"Thanks for telling me, Dad." I stood up and kissed him on the forehead. "And thanks for the pie. It was great."

"Sorry about the burned parts. There's butter in the crust, which can carry salmonella," he said. "Well, you knew that."

He ruffled my hair.

"Thanks for looking out for me."

He sighed. "You should probably stop searching for her, Sofia. I did. It's only going to make you sadder. Time to let her go."

"Okay, Dad."

He gave me a sad smile, and we both knew I wouldn't stop.

Chapter 9

Sure, I probably should have been focused on all the weird stuff that goes along with having a mummy for a boyfriend, or the fact that undead mummies existed at all. But really, I was too caught up with the fact that boyfriends existed. How were we going to deal with lunch plans? Would he have to drive me home after school? Should we hold hands in public? I'd never really examined my feelings on PDA. Sure, I hated it when other people did it, but it's different when it's you.

At the same time, I was irritated at myself for giving up everything else I was working on so I could think about him. I hadn't checked my notifications on Ancestry.com for over a week! What if there was a major declassifying of government documents? WHAT THEN?

The government would have to wait because there were other things to think about.

Sex, I mean. I tried to focus on other thoughts but somehow it snuck into every single one.

There were just so many things I didn't know about his

body. (Sex) How well preserved was he, exactly? (Sex? Sex.)

I mean, could he *do it* if he wanted to, assuming he wanted to, and specifically if he wanted to with me?

I mean, if the sex time was sex right and the sex situation presented its sex self... could we sex?

I know how this sounds. I'm really very sorry.

Hey, Brain. Hormones here. Oh yeah, we've met before. Remember swimming club? Never mind. Hey, I had a thought. How about instead of working on this assignment let's think about all our favorite parts of Seth and what they might taste like.

Maybe I'll just write his name on this notebook.

Oh geez. Now I have to destroy this page. And probably the next pages too just in case he does that thing where you rub the side of a pencil and see what was written on the page above. Will Dad be suspicious if I take a sudden interest in the paper shredder?

Hey, Brain. I know thinking is usually your area but I just had another idea. What if we Googled everything sexual we'd ever seen in a movie? No reason.

How about I'll learn everything there is to know about sex and then if it ever happens, I SAID IF, I'll be ready. Better to be prepared.

Sigh, good point, Brain. We'll use "incognito browsing mode." Glad I have you on my team.

Here's a question I can't Google: what does he expect from me? He could be 4,000 years old, he must have done everything a million times. Could I be good enough for him?

He told me I was the only girl he'd kissed, but he kissed like a guy who had done a lot of kissing. If he was that good at everything the first time he tried it, I was in good, chemically-preserved hands.

But if he's afraid of what the moisture of a kiss could

do to his corpse, what would happen if we—OH GOD I'M SO SORRY NOW I MADE YOU THINK ABOUT THAT TOO. UGHHHHHHH.

Cart, get back behind this horse. You're freaking everybody out up there.

For a couple weeks we saw each other every night. He would come over to "study" and we'd end up kissing in my room. He was so sure, so confident, even though I had to be careful not to put too much pressure on his fragile remains. He'd survived this long, I would hate for him to be crushed making out.

He'd drive home and call me from his car. Dad would not have approved of that, but I'd been trying not to think about his opinions as much recently.

We'd talk until we fell asleep.

I'm so self-conscious telling you this. In the moment it's all electricity and there's a slight humming in my ears and I feel like the world suddenly makes sense. Then later I think, "What did we even talk about that whole time? Movies, I think? And then eventually we were just making noises and giggling?" I'd feel okay if you wanted to vomit right now.

One Saturday we went for a long hike in the hills. I was hiking, he was more shuffling, but that's fine. I didn't really want to go very fast anyway. He had the cutest shuffle, actually. Mouth hung open a bit, right shoulder lower than the left. It was adorable.

When he seemed absorbed in the view, I'd try to mimic his walk just behind him, and then straighten up as soon as he noticed. He pretended to be angry but the whole time he'd be suppressing a laugh.

We sat on a rock so I could rest and rehydrate. He never got tired and definitely didn't want water, so I'd have to remind him that one of us was still mortal.

He rested his hand on my knee and electricity shot up my leg.

"Your skin is so soft," he said wistfully.

"Modern lotions are amazing," I bragged.

"When I was a kid, we had these servants who would anoint our whole bodies with oil before major religious services."

"Like a chicken wing."

"No, Princess. Like royalty."

"Potato/po-tah-to. So it wasn't gross?"

"No, my skin would feel amazing for weeks after."

"It'll definitely jinx everything to point this out, but this is the most you've talked about your childhood."

"It's hard, Sofia. I want to tell you all about it, but it's hard."

"Because it was so good it'll sound like you're showing off?"

"Hardly. You remember we didn't have toilets yet?"

"Oh yeah. Ugh."

"All the gold in the known world couldn't buy us the luxuries of your most disgusting room."

"A fair point."

I stroked the bandages on his hand, careful not to disturb them and hasten his decline.

He kissed me, gently at first and then more urgently.

Like the night of our first kiss, there was something in the air.

I brought my hand to his hips, letting him know I was ready if he was too. He stopped me.

"Sofia," he started. Then didn't finish.

It was happening again. More secrets. And things were

going so well.

"You've been so amazing but there's so much you don't know about me."

"Yeah, I know. That's why I'm slowly prying it out of you."

"But, you know, big stuff."

"I get that you're way more experienced than me, but I've done a ton of research and I'm a fast learner. I'll get better."

"What?"

"What?"

"What are you talking about, Princess?"

"What are *you* talking about?"

"I thought I was talking about the way we met, why I'm here. But I hadn't gotten to the part where I really share my past with you."

"Ohhhhhhh. That makes way more sense."

"And what were you talking about?"

"Nothing."

His hand was still on my hip, and he moved it to my waist and tickled me a little.

"Tell me."

"I can't!" I managed between giggles.

He let off and his hollow eye sockets looked up at me sweetly. "Please tell me?"

Brain, you're up. Time for a really clever lie. My mouth flooded and the deluge of fluids and words began.

"It's basically all I've thought about for a week. I've learned everything I can. You do NOT want to see my browser history. I mean, you can't, because I've been very careful about information security. But I've researched every aspect of sex I could think of, even though the information out there is SUPER contradictory—don't get me started—but I think I've gleaned enough to get started, I mean, if you wanted and the time was right, I'm not pressuring you or anything, and I definitely don't feel pressured, if anything, maybe a little under-pressured."

He was laughing so hard I was worried he might tumble down the hill.

I turned away and folded my arms, pouting. I had found a new low.

He hugged me and I didn't hug back.

"The best thing about you is I don't have to wonder what you're thinking about, because you don't think anything you don't say."

"I have lots of private thoughts. I'm thinking one right now and you have no idea."

"Is it about me naked?"

"Shut up!" I pushed him away.

"Sofia." His tone was soft.

"What?"

"Nothing. I like you, that's all."

"I like you, too."

"I can tell. And so can Google, apparently."

I laughed again and he laughed too.

"I don't know the physics of it, but trust me, I've thought about it a lot, too," he said, as our laughter died away. "But I don't really want my first time to be on a rock in the middle of the afternoon."

"Oh yeah. That would be weird. When I'm with you, I forget where I am I guess."

"I know the feeling."

I was beaming. He liked me. I might die.

"Wait, what do you mean your first time? If you tell me you've been saving yourself for 5,000 years, I won't believe you."

"I see," he said, tense again. "Sofia, I'm not as old as you think. Not really. I was 16 when I died, and then I got reanimated about 2 years ago, so emotionally I'm 18. And physically, hard to say. Preservation is good but not perfect. My best guess is closer to 5,000 years, but I don't think that matters. We're basically the same age. Which is good, really. Monster or no, if I was hundreds or thousands of years older than you this would be a really troubling relationship."

I nodded, but it was a lot to think about. Too much in fact. Much easier to not think about any of it. I packed my water bottle and stood up.

"We should head back before it gets dark."

He didn't say anything, but he shrugged and started shuffling down the hill.

"That was a lot of information, I know." He finally said.

"I'm deciding which part to ask about first. Obviously the internet is going to get a bunch of searches tonight about preservation techniques, but right now all I can think about is how sad it is you died at 16."

"I guess it is. It was pretty common back then. Really hard not to die, actually. We had some medicines, but remember doctors only started washing their hands in the last hundred years, so you can imagine how bad things were in the early 3,000s BC."

"So what did you die of? Infection? In battle defending the Pharaoh? Or was it a crocodile attack? Oh, I hope it was crocodile attack."

"There are no crocodiles in the Nile, only alligators."

"Really?"

"Yep."

"Well then I hope you were attacked by alligators."

"Why?"

"It's such a good story."

"I tripped."

"No."

"Sorry. Am I ruining your image of me?"

"Absolutely. Now I'm saving myself for a cooler mummy."

"That hurts. It really does."

"What did you trip over?"

"My uncle was a great pharaoh. Which made me... rich. We didn't really need to work, but I was always fascinated with the way temples and monuments were built. I'd been hanging out with Sanseht, the greatest architect alive at the time. He taught me everything that went into building: stone cutting, balance, proportionality. Everything. And I loved it. My family thought this was all below me; somebody of my rank should just get oiled up and sit around eating figs."

"Doesn't sound all bad."

"Doesn't it?"

"Ok, I guess it does. I get bored pretty easily, and I'm not much for oil or figs."

"One night, Sanseht was showing me the work on the base of a great sphinx, and I was comparing the stonework to one of his plans. I wasn't watching my footing, and I tripped. I hit my head, everything went black, and next thing I knew it was a couple years ago, and I was a resurrected mummy."

"That's so sad."

"Weird is a better word. Impossible would work too. You're very calm about the existence of magic."

"I guess. I've just always wanted magic to exist, so when you showed me you were a mummy, I was ready. Like some kids always assume they were adopted or that they'll get to be an astronaut one day even though they're not training to be an astronaut. Magic called, and I was waiting by the phone."

"And people say I'm weird because I'm technically dead."

"They're not wrong."

"Then maybe we're perfect for each other."

I smiled at this, but I wasn't ready to move on quite yet. "So wait. You died, you were brought back by some kind of magic. That means... you know what the afterlife is like!"

"Of course."

"So what happens?"

"Look, people have come up with lots of theories in the last 5,000 years--"

"WHICH ONE IS RIGHT?"

"As I was saying, people have come up with lots of theories. But they didn't need to because we nailed it back in ancient Egypt. You cross the river on a canoe made of bones, pay your toll, enter the world of the dead. Just like my people said. Everything else humans came up with after that was way off."

"That's amazing!"

He tried to hold it back, but a smile crept onto his face, and he burst out laughing. I looked at him confused.

"I'm messing with you, Princess. I have no idea what the afterlife is like."

"How can you not know?"

"I told you. I tripped, hit my head, and woke up in modern times. I have no memory of the in-between. It didn't feel like any time had passed. You know when you're about to fall asleep and then you suddenly jerk awake? That's how it was. One second I'm young and rich, then I blink, and the next thing I know... this."

"So you might have gone to the afterlife, but they wiped your memory when you came back."

"Sure."

"Or maybe there's nothing."

"Could be."

"Or maybe you didn't get to go to heaven so you don't know."

"Also possible."

"It's official. I'm saving myself for a mummy who actually remembers the afterlife."

I ran off ahead of him.

He yelled after me, "That's tough, but fair. Goodbye forever!"

We got back to the house. Dad was just putting the finishing scorch on Burger Night.

"Princess, Seth. Glad you made it back. Everything okay on your hike?"

"It was just fine," I said. Seth was still slightly out of breath, but he nodded as well.

"No snakes?"

"No snakes."

"Did you know you can Mace a snake?"

"You mentioned that, yeah, Dad. Pretty sure you're wrong about that, but you did mention it."

"I didn't say it was ethical, or even that it was effective, just that it was physically possible."

Seth chuckled. Dad was happy to have a new audience for his dad jokes.

"Staying for dinner, Prince Seth?"

Seth flinched a tiny bit about being called a prince, but Dad didn't seem to notice. "No, sir. Very kind offer but I have some work to finish up at home."

"Good man. We should go bowling next week. The three of us."

"That sounds delightful, sir."

"That's definitely not happening," I cut in. "Come on, Seth. I'll walk you out."

"Want me to get rid of her, Seth?" Dad yelled after us. "We can hang out, just the two of us?"

"DAD!"

Seth laughed again. "Nice guy."

"He's the worst," I corrected.

Seth kissed me lightly.

"You don't have to go. You could stay for Burn Burgers and then we could 'study' after dinner."

"How about this. You do some actual studying after dinner so you don't fall behind in your classes, and after your dad goes to bed I'll sneak back in, and we can not even pretend to study."

I nodded, and before my mouth could ruin everything with saliva or talking, he hopped in his car and drove off.

I went inside to eat and do some last minute research, just in case anything had changed.

Chapter 10

This was supposed to be the sex chapter.

This was going to be the part where I told you about all the amazing things that happened after Seth came over, or, more likely, the part where I politely refused to tell you the details but heavily implied some things.

But here's a complete description of what happened: I waited, and Seth never showed up.

There was lots of frantic texting. Some light crying. And eventually I fell asleep, absolutely miserable.

I could think of two possible explanations.

Explanation #1

Seth was at home reading *Crime and Punishment* for his English final when he heard a noise in the kitchen. He went to investigate and as he did, Bunny the Grave Robber smashed through the back door, knocking over his canister of single origin coffee beans—wait, was he actually a hipster too, or just a mummy? I'd never asked him. Either way he probably couldn't do any liquids, but he'd keep coffee around for guests.

Eli rushed in behind him with a shovel or a pickaxe. Probably a burlap sack too.

Seth was faster and sexier than any grave robber, though, so he was ready. He grabbed a vinyl record off the shelf (Tom Waits' *Closing Time*, if I had to venture a guess) and hucked it like a frisbee, catching Bunny in the ankle, bringing him to the ground on top of the finest coffee the world had ever known, now wasted thanks to this careless brute.

Eli was smarter and maybe a bit wilier. He took one look around Seth's immaculate and tastefully decorated retro chic kitchen and grabbed a Santoku knife from the bamboo knife block, tossing the blade menacingly from hand to hand.

"Where are my manners?" Seth probably said, coolly. "I forgot to offer you something to drink!"

And with that he picked up the hammered bronze tea kettle and clocked the grave robber right in the temple. Eli's hands went slack, and he dropped the knife... and the shovel... and the pickaxe, I guess. And the burlap sack, too. Point is, whatever he was still holding, he dropped when Seth tea-kettled him.

Seth ripped some gauze off his arm and tied them up. Did he have enough gauze to just use it like that, or would he tie them up with the twine that hipsters always have lying around for crafty gifts and wedding decorations? He'd probably use the twine.

What Seth didn't suspect, though, was that after their defeat at the Desert King's Mini Golf Course, Bunny and Eli wouldn't attack alone. Three more grave robbers—who I don't have time to make up names for—rushed in while Seth was making his perfect twine handcuffs. Seth dropped his crafting scissors, but not before one of the robbers smashed him on the head with a shovel and the other two hoisted him into the burlap sack. Then they threw some coffee beans in the faces of their two friends who woke up grumbling, and the five of them dragged Seth out and threw him in the back of their unmarked grave-robbing van, thus preventing Seth from coming over to my house for sex.

OR.

Explanation #2, and the one that seemed far more likely in my current self-centered state

It became obvious to Seth that I'd be terrible at sex, so he decided to go find somebody cooler/prettier/more experienced/generally better.

Yeah, that was probably it.

Chapter 11

There's only one way to deal with your first ever boyfriend skipping out on your planned illicit meeting: yoga pants.

He hadn't answered my texts for three days, and my loungewear was starting to smell. My dad called me Princess Mopey once, and I was so busy feeling sorry for myself I couldn't even think of a better comeback than, "That makes you King Mopey, technically, because that's how royal lineage works."

Duncan didn't have a chance to call me names because I'd been ignoring him. I'd shut off all contact until I figured out what it was about me that was so gross that a beautiful boy who seemed to like me would run screaming from the thought of getting closer to me. If he thought I was disgusting, then I was going to show him. I was going to be even more disgusting than he thought.

Then on the fourth day something changed. I realized that moping was super duper boring. Anybody who dealt with a breakup, even one as shocking as mine, by sitting around feeling sorry for themselves forever might have deserved to be dumped in the first place.

I needed to get out of the house but I wasn't quite ready to give up on my comfy pants, so I signed up for a kickboxing class.

My dad had always been trying to get me to learn self-defense, and since there were now actual enemies trying to rob me, it seemed like as good a time as any.

I didn't buy Seth's theory about leading the grave robbers away from me since they'd attacked me the one time he was mysteriously out of town. Maybe he had his own problem with them, but these guys were definitely after me. They knew my name and exactly where to find me. By running away from me he'd just left me alone and unprotected.

I found an ad online for classes at Punchy Jim's Punching Gym (and Laundromat) where the first session was always free and so was drying. That's a business plan I could get behind. I hoped this Punchy fellow could teach me how to protect myself against any attackers, but especially those wielding sporting equipment.

Punchy was huge. 6 foot 50, if he was an inch. He had a shaved head and a vein bulging out of his forehead, and apparently he didn't believe in sleeves. Or maybe humans just hadn't invented sleeves big enough to contain his hulking muscles, which were the size of Duncans. To clarify, not the size of Duncan's muscles; the size of *multiple Duncans*, up till this point the biggest person I'd ever seen up close.

And while he was welcoming in his words, he talked quickly with the intensity of a propane torch.

The first class only had three people in it. I was partnered with Becky, a single mother of two who had hoped this class would be great for meeting guys. Tina, a blonde pixie police detective, had to spar with Punchy, which would have been unfair were it not for the content of the first lesson.

"There are several theories of self defense, but everybody agrees: guys don't like being kicked in the balls."

We spent almost an hour on the technique for ball kicking and since we were all women, we had to take turns pretending to have balls. In other contexts, that would probably be more fun.

The second half of class was focused on eye gouging because, as Punchy said, "eyes are the balls of the face."

He promised us lots of good biting/scratching if we came back. He wasn't concerned about form as much as efficiency, which I liked.

As we were leaving, I asked if he had any specific advice for mini-golf related attacks.

"A golf club is a melee weapon, but it's also got a bit of range. Too far away to kick him in the balls. You've got two main choices: run, and pepper spray."

"I've got a favorite brand," I said, showing him the small can attached to my backpack.

"Hey, the Desert King's own. You know your pepper spray."

"My dad raised me right."

"I'll say," he said, approvingly. "Now quick, that dummy over there is running at you. What do you do?"

I kicked it square in the crotch and gouged its eyes. A bell dinged. I felt better already.

Back at home, my yoga pants were so sweaty I had to take them off. I showered and put on some people clothes, which meant I was 90% of the way back to the world of the not-moping.

The next logical step was to try to get my friends back.

I texted Duncan when I was outside his place rather than ringing the doorbell and risking his dad answering. It wasn't that Duncan's dad was bad or anything, quite the opposite. His kindness and stories were both unending. If I saw him, it'd be an hour before I got around to apologizing, and I wasn't sure my nerve would last.

As I waited on the porch, I browsed Duncan's collection of historical artifacts. There wasn't room in the Cavolo residence for all of Dunc's treasures, so they left most of them on the porch, despite the fact that they were mostly phalluses.

Oh jeez, I haven't even mentioned the phallus thing yet, have I? I'm so sorry, it's just something that I've known for so long I forget to tell people sometimes. Duncan has North America's biggest collection of ancient stone phalluses.

I know, I know. It sounds insane, but here's what happened: A younger but still giant Duncan is just getting into amateur archeology. He's interning at a Coso dig site when he comes across this ancient fertility statue. His first ever academic find and it's a dong. That's what it is.

Mini Duncan is proud of his first discovery, but he's too embarrassed to tell his supervisors about it. Finally he goes onto his amateur digger message board and talks about how "hypothetically" he might have found something like this and what should he do, and the older members think it's funny he's so squeamish, so they play a little joke on him by sending him a couple castings of ancient phalluses they've discovered. Before you know it, he's got a reputation as the guy who you send your phalluses to.

It was kindof a mean thing, but Dunc is so good natured, he just decided to roll with it. After that, well, if you tell everybody you collect bottle openers, people send you every bottle opener they come across.

"You're not dead," Duncan said as he opened the door, not entirely thrilled about the discovery.

"You either! In fact, that's the first thing I notice about most people," I said, pretending we were having fun. We weren't.

I felt a little bad about how I'd treated Duncan. After he'd confided in me about his steroid addiction (I think), he got a pretty serious concussion. Then I dropped him off at the hospital and kinda sorta didn't talk to him at all for a few weeks. I felt more than a little bad. "A lot bad" wouldn't be overstating it, but it would be bad grammar.

"What happened to your boyfriend?"

He stayed near the door, resting his hand on a full-scale replica of a 6-foot-tall Incan phallus inscribed with prayers for plentiful pregnancies.

"I'm here because you're my best friend, Dunc. Even when I'm not holding up my end of the friendship."

"Do you love him?"

"I like him," I hedged. "A lot."

Love might be a little sudden. He was my first boyfriend, and I was his first girlfriend in thousands of years. If this wasn't time for caution, I didn't know what was.

"What's so special about him?" he asked, and his normally buoyant voice wobbled.

I sighed and steadied myself on a 4-foot ceremonial wang from Easter Island. The pedestal it was on had hand-carved drawings of rituals that, if I'm being honest, looked intriguing.

This wasn't the place for secrets.

"He's a mummy," I said. "And I like him. Even though he ran away from me."

"I've known you since you were a child," he responded, "and I'll never run away from you because I love you."

I almost knocked over the Easter Islander.

"What? No, Duncan. You don't love me."

"Hey. I can accept that you don't feel the same way at the moment but you can't tell me what I feel," he said, righting the phallus on its stand and shooing me away from it.

"Okay," I said. "I don't feel the same way."

"I can't accept that!"

"But you just said--"

"Look, you might love him more but--"

"Like."

"Whatever. Like. But I'm better for you."

My head was swimming.

"Wait, so this is about a love triangle and not about you doing steroids?"

"Yes. Why is that so hard to accept?"

"It literally never occurred to me that Princess Beige would ever be in a love triangle."

"It's really more like a love angle since Seth and I aren't also dating. It's just two lines pointing toward you."

"That makes sense geometrically, I guess. Except Sofia's 1st law is that no lines ever point toward me."

"Sofia, you are so smart about everything besides judging people, and that includes yourself. You don't have any idea how special you are."

"I think you're special too, just not in that way."

"You've known Seth, what? A month? You've known me your whole life, and I've never left your side."

"I don't know how to explain it to you, Duncan. You're such a good friend... there's just something different with him. Something electric. He gets me. He cares about me. He thinks I'm funny."

"I think you're funny."

"I'm sorry, Duncan, but you're not going to talk me into having feelings."

"I know. I just want you to see." He ran his hand through his hair, trying to find the right words.

"Why didn't you ever tell me you liked me?"

"Love. And I tried but you never got it. You always assumed I was talking about something else, like steroids."

"So you've never taken them?"

"A couple times freshman year when I was trying to make the baseball team, but I stopped."

"It doesn't look like it."

"Stop changing the subject. Wait a second. Did you say he was a mummy?"

"Like an hour ago. I wondered if you were ever going to notice."

"I rehearsed this conversation for 10 years. I didn't plan for all the variables, apparently."

"I was surprised, too, when I found out."

Duncan cocked his head and squinted at me. "A mummy. What do you mean he's a mummy?"

"Like a preserved corpse. Thousands of years old. You know, a mummy."

"Like that Brendan Fraser movie?"

"In that, that is a movie featuring a mummy, yes."

"How do you know?"

"What do you mean how do I know? He told me. Besides, it's pretty obvious if you think about it. The bandages, the way his mouth hangs open, the shuffle-walk, the acrid smell of sand and chemicals."

"Huh. I just assumed he was, like, a hipster."

"I know! But he's not. Or at least, he's not *just* a hipster. He's definitely a mummy."

"You just never know about people."

"Tell me about it."

"This doesn't change anything, Sof. It's him or me."

"Him."

"Stop choosing him over me!"

"Stop making me choose!"

He took a couple careful steps toward me, his hands up in defeat.

"Look, Sofia. I get it. He's mysterious. He makes you feel special. He's a reanimated remnant of ancient Egypt and he's got a great hoodie. He's seen the world, or at least he would have if they hadn't removed his eyes and preserved them separately."

"Oh yeah. I'll have to ask him about that."

"But I just don't see you two together. If you want a guy who's going to nail the passionate romance part and then get you clubbed by goons, then great. Go for him."

"I choose that, yeah."

"No, I'm not done."

"Yeah?"

"But Sofia, I actually know you. We hang out and talk about dumb stuff. I'm a living human your own age. That's a huge thing right there: I'm alive. Isn't that something you look for in a boyfriend? And anyway, he ran away from you. I'm here."

"You're still trying to talk me into this. I don't know what's happening with Seth right now but that doesn't mean I'm going to just run into your arms."

We were interrupted by a giant white bird with a black head flying overhead and squawking.

"That's weird," Duncan said, distracted.

"Weird is pretty much where we're at, yeah."

"Sorry, Sof."

"What do you want me to do with any of this?"

"Whatever you want." He flopped into a stone chair

carved out of stylized curving phalluses from the Ming Dynasty and shrugged. "But I couldn't keep acting like I didn't feel something when I did."

"That's fair, Duncan," I said. "But I can't act like I feel something when I don't."

He looked defeated.

"Should I go?"

"Run back to your mummy."

"I wish I could. I don't know where he is."

"Well you know where I am if you ever change your mind."

I'd gotten a boyfriend and then lost him AND my best friend at the same time. I turned to leave. I had to weave between a couple of marble pillars that were, unsurprisingly very long phalluses. Apparently they held up the roof of an ancient Greek brothel. I navigated them successfully, regrouped, and continued to storm off.

Chapter 12

The next day it was only Tina and me at kickboxing class. To test our strength, we took turns wailing on the dummy's crotch with our knees. His name was BIFF which probably stood for something but given what we were doing to him, it seemed like a weird time to get to know him.

BIFF was electronic and had five different calibrations of yowl. By the end of the workout I was still only getting a level four.

"I feel like you're stopping short," said Tina. "Try to drive your knee through the back of BIFF's spine."

"Won't that hurt me too?" I asked.

Tina shrugged. "Yes, but not as much as it'll hurt him. Kneecaps can take some punishment and dish out a whole lot more. Right, Punchy?"

"Never leave home without 'em," he said. "If you're always worried about getting hurt, Princess, you'll never be able to truly hurt others."

I shuddered. "Sometimes I feel like everybody in my life speaks in metaphors, and that's not even a good one."

"No metaphor intended. I meant that very literally about knees and nuts."

Punchy smiled, then got distracted by something behind me. I turned slowly and was shocked to see, standing outside the window of Punchy Jim's Punching Gym, staring directly at me, a beautiful black and white bird. Combined with the one I had seen the day before, it made for a grand total of two sightings of these birds in a week, which beat my previous record of zero.

Even if they liked this area, which I doubted, they definitely weren't a city bird. But for some reason this one looked like he was shopping for martial arts classes.

"Ooh, is that an African sacred ibis?" Tina asked.

"If it is, he's a long way from home," Punchy added.

"Definitely. They prefer marshy wetlands and mudflats. Also, they prefer Africa."

"But that black plumage around its head and on the tips of its wings, it's unmistakable. Same size and shape as an egret but that color pattern is unique to the ibis."

"There aren't a lot of frogs or fish around here for him to eat. I bet he's hungry. Poor guy."

"What, are you all amateur ornithologists?" I asked incredulously.

"We have a club," said Tina.

"It meets on Wednesdays," Punchy added. "In case you're free."

Man, I am terrible at judging people.

When I didn't respond, Tina piped up again. "We should call the Audubon Society. I'm worried about its safety."

I started toward the door, mesmerized. Every step I took, it followed with its head.

"Slow down there, Princess," said Punchy Jim. "You don't want to go near that thing."

Without breaking eye contact, it walked over to the door and tapped it twice with its beak. When we didn't move, it almost looked annoyed, and tapped again. Then it slowly lifted its right leg and pointed with its beak at a yellow tube tied to it.

"What have you got there, little guy?" Punchy was the only one who could charitably call the bird little. It was one full me, or about a third of a him.

He opened the door and the bird took a step inside, still looking annoyed.

The tube was now clearly a scroll wrapped around its bony ankle. Do birds have ankles? Whatever, it had a scroll there.

Tina approached and lifted the ibis's leg up to take off the scroll.

"It looks like papyrus which, even for an Egyptian bird, seems weird," she said uncertainly.

My heart was in my throat.

"Oh!" she said, handing me the scroll. "It's for you, Sofia."

I thanked her and grabbed it tentatively. I hadn't received a written letter since my Aunt Ginny stopped sending me birthday cards in the 6th grade, and I was pretty sure I'd never gotten one delivered by bird. Maybe my family's just terrible at keeping in touch.

I unrolled it and read while Punchy excitedly noted the bird's features to Tina.

> *My Dear Sofia,*
> *Despite what you probably think, I didn't abandon you for somebody cooler, smarter, or prettier because no such person exists. Also because I was kidnapped.*

My captors insisted I write a letter asking you to come and save me. If you try, they will surely kill you. You know I can never let that happen, so I've secretly replaced that letter with this one.

Whatever you do, don't come looking for me.

I'm sorry, but it's better this way. Twice now I've led them to you, and I won't do that again, under any circumstances.

If you never see me again, just know that I am happy because I've done everything I can to make sure you are safe, and that my long life was finally worth something because I knew you. Is that too dramatic? Well, deal with it. Being kidnapped is a pretty intense thing, and I'm feeling dramatic at the moment.

Eventually they will come looking for you again, so you need to hide. Get away from there. I know it will be hard to leave your family and friends, but your life depends on it. Don't tell anybody you're leaving. Just go.

Well, there is one person you should tell. I don't have time to explain all of this, but there's a woman who will know how to make you disappear. You'll find her at the Red Roof Inn on Commercial Drive.

Please stay safe. I love you.

-Seth

P.S.: This is an ibis. He's a good friend of mine. His name is Khu, which means The Protector. It was a long flight for him to get to you, so he would probably appreciate a couple of small fish or a frog if you have one handy.

Tina whistled. I frowned at her for reading over my shoulder, but I couldn't blame her.

"Princess, what did you get mixed up in?"

"I fell in love with a mummy."

"Reanimated mummies are real?" she asked, not as surprised as I would have expected.

"Sure they are," said Punchy Jim. "Covered in bandages, smell like sage and sand. I trained with one in Thailand last time I was over there. Went by Raymond. Wasn't strong, but for a 2,000 year old, he sure was spry."

"Does that mean unicorns and mermaids are real too?"

"I'm pretty sure it's just mummies," Punchy said.

"That's still cool."

I sank to the floor, holding the papyrus with one hand, burying my face in the other.

"I'm never going to be able to rescue him."

"Well," Punchy suggested reasonably, "maybe that's why he told you not to."

"But I have to at least try. Will you help me?"

I looked back and forth between them. Tina kicked the ground and rubbed the back of her neck.

"Look, honey. I like you. But I've got enough going on in my own life. Nothing personal."

"Me too," Punchy said, somewhat ashamed. "I'm a small business owner, you know. I can't just leave. No paid vacations in this line of work."

"But what do I do?"

"I see a problem, I kick it in the balls. But some problems you can't kick in the balls, Sofia. And those problems I stay away from entirely. You should too, if you know what's best for you."

"Maybe you should take his advice," added Tina. "Find this mystery lady at the Red Roof and disappear."

Khu the ibis made a clucking sound from somewhere deep in his elongated throat.

"But whatever you do, first you have to find this guy some fish."

I stormed out of the gym and Khu followed faithfully behind me.

After picking up some herring from Whole Foods, I went to Duncan's house. He hadn't done great in our last fight with the grave robbers but it was him or my dad and I didn't think these guys were going to take a break from being evil long enough to discuss things over burnt pie. And after the Macing I gave that one, he'd have goggles on when I showed up for sure.

Duncan was on his porch dusting a fossilized Native American phallus about the size of a Maglight.

I startled him when I tapped him on the shoulder, which in turn startled Khu, who clucked at him in distaste.

He looked ready to start another fight with me, but then he noticed something was wrong.

"What's going on, Sofia? And why is an African sacred ibis following you around? He's going to need to get back to a marshy wetland and fast."

"How does everybody know more about birds than me?"

"Audubon Club on Wednesdays at Marianne's house. I've literally invited you a dozen times," he sniffed.

"Look, I need your help, not another hobby. Seth disappeared before we could... I mean Seth's been kidnapped."

"What? How do you know?"

"He sent me a surprisingly thorough note on a piece of papyrus attached to Khu's leg." I gestured at the ibis who nodded slightly, as if glad to be properly introduced.

"I guess that answers my other question. But jeez, Khu,

you flew all the way from Egypt? Did this mean lady at least give you some frogs?"

Khu clucked at him.

"All I could find was herring."

"Psh. I guess that'll do but they like frogs better."

"Great, next time I'm at the live frog store, I'll pick some up."

"You don't have to be snippy at me just because you're a terrible caretaker for this magnificent bird."

"Point taken. But if we can stay on track here, Duncan, Seth was kidnapped by the same thugs who attacked us at that evil tiny golf course."

He bristled. "I hate those guys as much as anybody, but that doesn't mean I'm going across the world to save your boyfriend from them."

"They gave you a concussion."

"Maybe I had it coming. I was taking my sweet time on that third hole."

"You're not going to help me either? I guess I have no friends left."

He softened a little but not all the way.

"I'm sorry, Sofia, but I'm not going to risk my life just to make it easier for you to be with somebody else. I have a whole life ahead of me digging in the dirt, expanding this fine collection," he waved his hand over his 100+ stone phalluses tenderly, "and getting over you."

I waited a moment before delivering my final blow.

"They're grave robbers."

"WHAT." His hand gripped a curved Sumerian member with intricate carvings at the base.

"The thugs. They want a jewel or something."

I handed over the note. At first he looked concerned but it turned to anger.

"Love? He loves you? How long have you known him, like 10 minutes?"

"I'm sure he meant to say 'like' but he's been kidnapped. He must have panicked."

He crossed his arms and leaned against the house, clearly weighing all this in his head.

"I'm sorry, Duncan. I know this is hard for you, but I don't know where else to turn. They're going to kill him if we don't find him. I can't let that happen, and I'm not going to just run away from my dad and hide." I reached over and touched his shoulder. "And I'm not going to run away from you. Even though it might not feel like it, I really care about you."

"Sofia, this IS hard for me. Harder than you'll ever know. But in the end, I think I want you to be happy more than anything. Tell me what you want to do and I'll help."

I jumped and hugged him around his beefy neck.

"Oh thank you, Duncan!"

"Plus I hate graverobbers with a fiery passion."

"Great, let's go."

"Wait, where are we going?"

"Oh, good question."

"I guess we need to find that woman, right?"

"Right. We'll just tell her we don't actually need her help escaping but that she needs to tell us where Seth might be."

"And if she won't talk, we'll make her talk."

"Calm down there, Mr. Interrogator. Let's go with subtle first."

Duncan and I approached the front desk nervously. The woman working there saw Duncan and smiled broadly.

"Excuse me," I said as innocently as I could muster. "I

hate to complain but there's a giant bird bathing himself in the pool and it's frightening the children."

"What?" She rushed to the window. "Oh God, is that an African sacred ibis? What's he doing all the way over here? We need to rescue it, this is totally the wrong climate."

Jesus. This club must be really good.

"That's what I thought too, Nicole," Duncan said to the attendant. "I think that's why it went straight for the pool. But the chlorine could kill it."

"Oh dear. Okay, will you call the Audubon Society? There are some frogs who live in the bushes out back. I'll go grab a couple to lure him out of the pool."

She rushed off. Duncan pulled out his phone and chased after her.

I tried to look like I was just interested in the complimentary *USA Today* as I leaned further and further over the counter. Nicole's computer screen wasn't locked and the menu included a "guest list" option. I looked around in what was probably the most suspicious manner possible and, seeing nobody, clicked it.

I scanned names furiously, searching for any clue as to who might be here that could help me. Would she have a name that gave her away? What was I even looking for?

Before long I heard Duncan's voice from the hallway. He was talking louder than he needed to, probably to warn me I was almost out of time.

Crap. I got to the bottom of the list of names and did a double take.

There it was. Room #419. Tia. Murdoch. She was still using my dad's last name.

Chapter 13

She was here.

She was supposed to be in Morocco or in jail or in space or dead or dead in a Moroccan space jail. Anywhere but a freaking Red Roof Inn! She could've come back anytime she wanted, but she'd rather spend $40 a night to stay just outside of town.

I was still in shock as Duncan and the clerk re-entered the lobby. They were chatting about the differences between the ibis and the common heron.

"Thanks again for your help, Nicole. I just didn't want to see any harm come to such a beautiful creature."

"Of course, Duncan. I'm just glad it's safe. I'll see you Wednesday?"

"Are you bringing more of that banana bread?"

She giggled. "Not this week. Jeff is in charge of snacks."

"Too bad."

Is this what flirting looks like? Go, Duncan, go!

As soon as we were outside, Duncan swung me around into a piggyback. It momentarily distracted me from my whole life turning upside down.

"Jeez, Dunc. Is this what the world looks like to you? How do you not spend most of your time admiring the view?"

"It's difficult, but humans can get used to anything."

We rounded the side of the building, and he was almost skipping. "What a rush! We just pulled off a caper! We're such a good team, Sof."

He ducked behind some bushes near a side entrance and reality crashed back around me. I was too exhausted to even respond.

"What is it, Princess? What did you find? Is she here? Who is she, this mysterious woman who can help us fight evil? I hope she's like a ninja or something."

I could barely whisper the words into his ear.

"My mom."

"Your mom? What about her?"

"It was her name. She's in room 419. She's here, Duncan. Here is where she is."

He almost dropped me, but caught himself, and slowly lowered me to the ground.

"Your mom is here? She can't be here. That doesn't make any sense."

"That's exactly what I'm saying. She can't be here. But she is. I looked it up, and databases don't lie."

"That's intense."

"I've been searching for her for years and now she's in a crappy motel in town."

"So you think she's our secret ninja?"

"She has to be. Which only makes things weirder because my mummy boyfriend somehow knew she was here. How did he know that? Whatever's going on, I'm not sure I can handle it."

"Whoa there, Sof. I know it's a lot to take in, but you've wanted to see your mom for ages. If I can handle you not being in love with me, then you can handle getting the one thing you've always wanted."

He had a point but that somehow made me feel worse.

Duncan walked over to the side door and reached for the handle. "Let's go, Princess. We're doing this."

I grabbed his arm.

"Wait. What do I do? What do I say to her?"

"I don't know, but maybe start with, 'What the hell is going on?' See where it goes from there."

"Why is everything so simple to you?"

"Why is everything so complicated to you?"

"This isn't really a pep talk, but your condescension is actually just what I needed. I'm glad you're here, Duncan." I let go of his arm.

"Me too. Now go get 'em, tiger."

He held the door open, and I gave a pitiful "rawr" as I walked by.

I stood at the door to room 419, deciding if I should go for a shy knock or a falsely confident one when the door opened and saved me the trouble.

It was dark inside, and I couldn't quite make out the figure in the doorway.

"Princess Sofia."

The voice made my insides churn.

"Mom?"

"Hurry up and close the door, we don't need to air condition the whole desert."

"Mom!" I rushed in and hugged her, not even trying to hold back the eruption of tears.

She hugged me tightly, and I took in her smell. Just like

old times.

"I love you so much, Sofia. You have to know that."

She cried. Then she hugged Duncan, whom she probably didn't recognize as my formerly scrawny friend who used to play house with me in our backyard, but it was a hugging time.

Duncan was crying too.

Mom handed around tissues, and I sat on one bed while she took the edge of the other. Duncan leaned on the desk, wiping his eyes.

Mom looked great. Part of me hoped she'd withered with all the angry thoughts I sent into the universe after her, but apparently hate vibes are good for your skin. Or she uses some kind of SPF 50 hatescreen.

She had the same high cheekbones and angular eyebrows, her dark brown hair falling in waves around her face. And she was impeccably dressed with an airy scarf and big earrings.

I looked her over and over, memories flooding back. I assumed at any moment she'd start to explain everything, but she didn't.

Finally she mustered a single sentence, sounding exhausted. "I'm sorry, honey."

"So did you ever get that pack of cigarettes?"

"Don't think I'm missing your tone, young lady," she said with a hint of a smile. Mom always seemed to enjoy my sarcasm, though some unwritten parental rule required her to be critical of it.

Suddenly it all became too much. "What the hell, Mom? I mean seriously, what the hell? Why did you leave? Where did you go? Why are you back? What does any of this have to do with Seth? How long have you been at this stupid motel?" A tiny hole had been poked in the tank of my emotions and now they were shooting out. "I've got a million questions but all of them fall under the general umbrella of WHAT THE HELL, MOM???"

She looked down sadly and played with her bracelet.

After a bit, she tried to talk. "I need you to understand, Sofia, I never wanted to leave you, but I had to. To protect you."

"I've been getting an awful lot of that recently, and I don't like it. Apparently nobody's come up with a way to protect me without ripping my heart out first."

"I had to."

"How about teaching me to look out for myself? How about explaining anything to me at any point? How about at least having the decency to say goodbye?"

"I didn't have a choice, honey."

"You always have a choice."

As happy as I was to see her, I couldn't hide the anger that I'd been harboring for years. Years of coming home to an empty house, staring wistfully out the window, searching every database on the internet for clues about what I did wrong to drive her away, the acrid smell of burnt pancakes, all of it.

"Sofia."

She moved next to me and put an arm around my shoulder. She was fighting back tears again.

"I deserve this. I deserve all of this. You're right, I had a choice. I made a bad one. I'll regret that for the rest of my life. But I *felt* like I didn't. I thought I was doing the right thing, the right thing for you and your father. I was afraid my past mistakes would come back and hurt you."

I softened a little. It never occurred to me that she would actually feel bad about all this.

"Please, Sofia. I need you to forgive me."

After a second of trying to hold my ground I crumbled

and leaned over and hugged her as hard as I could.

"I'm just so glad to see you again, Mom. I have a million things to tell you."

"I have a million questions. And plenty to tell you as well."

Duncan was squirming. "You know, um, I'm going to, you know, get some ice from the ice machine. In case we need ice."

Mom and I laughed.

"Please stay here, Duncan," she said kindly. "I still need to protect my little girl, but I can't do it alone. She needs as many people who love her as possible, and you're one of those. I need you to hear this too."

He leaned back again, still not looking entirely comfortable but somewhat flattered that she remembered him.

"I think the most important thing to tell you both is who I am, and by extension, who you are, Sofia."

"Well, I know some of that. I know a lot about your family tree."

"How far back?"

"Five generations, give or take?"

"That's pretty impressive. But I'm talking way before that."

"Really?" I leaned forward on my elbows, unable to hide how exciting that was. "How far back? Eight generations? Ten?"

"Thousands of years."

"Is this the princess thing Dad mentioned? There's no real way to verify that, I mean the record keeping just a hundred years ago gets pretty shoddy, how could you even expect--"

She cut me off.

"Not royalty, no. Sofia, you and I are both descended

from Anuket, the great Egyptian river goddess."

I stopped short. I looked at Duncan then back at her. Then back at Duncan. He shrugged.

"What?"

"The Nile Goddess, Anuket. One of the earliest Egyptian deities. Her mother was the goddess Satis, so technically we're descended from her too, but it's kinda fuzzy whether it was a real mother-daughter thing or more like 'from the same mud they were all born' thing."

"Of course," said Duncan, knowledgeably. His bravado covered how out of our depth we both felt.

"So we're goddesses?"

"Not exactly. We're descendants of the goddess and her people. We're like demigods, but lots of generations later."

"So demi demi demi demi gods?"

"Something like that, yeah."

"So we're mortal? That's a disappointment."

"Tell me about it. In fact, I broke my wrist a couple years ago. Wasn't doing anything exciting, just leaving a Starbucks, and I tripped over my own feet and tried to save the coffee, and ended up catching all my weight on one wrist. So stupid. So mortal."

"Oh my God, I've tripped over my own feet so many times!"

She smiled. It was so good to be with her again, but I was still so confused.

"So what do we actually get for being these demi-demis? Are we like people who claim they're 1/32 Cherokee or something? Are we being racist again?"

"Nothing like that. We still have the goddess's blood in our veins."

"Creepy," said Duncan. Mom shot him a look.

She continued. "We have some powers, some rights,

some responsibilities. And we've got *this*."

She pulled her necklace out from her shirt and I saw a beautiful blue stone set in an elaborate gold setting. She took it off, and I was mesmerized as it sparkled even in this dull motel light.

"Princess, this is your birthright: the River Jewel."

I was stunned staring at it.

"Here." She tried to toss it to me but the chain caught on her finger and the throw veered wide right, smashing into the mirror, cracking it, and exploding the jewel into a million tiny, beautiful shards.

"Mom! You broke the River Jewel!"

Duncan looked like he was about to pass out.

"Oops. Well, it's fine," she said dismissively. She hummed four notes and the Jewel reformed itself on the ground. "See? Good as new. Never was much for throwing sports."

"Me too! God, I've missed you, Mom."

"What about the mirror?" asked Duncan.

"Meh, it's a motel." She shrugged. "Anyway, the ancients believed it has the power to bring the dead back to life, just like the annual floods of the Nile brought life to the desert. And as you saw, its power can also fix that which is broken. Really handy little thing, actually."

"Okay, then seriously, you should fix the mirror."

Mom glared at Duncan, then sighed. She hummed the same four notes and the crack in the mirror slowly faded until it was completely gone.

"But its power can only be harnessed by somebody in whom the blood of the Anuket flows."

"So I can use it to fix stuff? That's great! I break plates all the time."

"Works on wrists too, I'm proud to say. But it'll take

time for you to learn how to focus its power."

Duncan gasped. "This must be what the grave robbers were looking for!"

"That's right," my mom said. "I knew they'd come eventually. That's why I took it and went into hiding. There are terrible people who would use its power for their own gain."

"I'm sure."

"No, honey, I mean real assholes."

"Okay?"

"He calls himself The Priest because he thinks he's so cool, though his real name is Harold. I thought if he were looking for me and the Jewel, he'd never come for you. But obviously I was wrong."

"Where does Seth fit into all this?"

"Let's say he's related to Harold."

Duncan shot up. "I knew it!"

"Calm down, Dunc," my mom said. "I didn't say *he's* an asshole. Seth is one of the sweetest people, er, well, *anythings* that I've ever met. Harold sent him to find me and bring me back, but he found you first instead and something about you changed his mind. He vowed never to help The Priest again. When he finally tracked me down, he offered me a truce. Since we both wanted to protect you from these other forces, it made sense. We've only talked a few times but he's really down to earth for a reanimated corpse."

"I can't help feeling a bit dirty about you becoming secret friends with my boyfriend."

"Why? I didn't tell him any embarrassing stories about you as a kid. Well, not many."

I tried to act offended, but I was just so happy to have my mom back and to know a bit more about why she left that I couldn't pull it off.

"But sadly, he spent too much time around you, and he acted like a beacon for the bad people who wanted to find you."

"The grave robbers."

"Yep. I tried to protect you both as best as I could."

"The army of cats at the mini-golf course? That was you?"

She gave a modest nod.

"I called in a favor. One of Bast's descendants, you know, the god of cats. He was happy to help out since everybody hates grave robbers. And honestly, that was the first time his power to summon a bunch of cats in a hurry actually helped."

"Man, I could have used that power earlier. I'm trying to make a viral video."

"Let me know next time, and I'll help out." She stroked my hair lovingly, and I was so happy I could burst. But something was still bothering me.

"I get that you wanted to protect me, and Seth wanted to protect me, but I just wish somebody trusted me with some information. How can I ever learn to defend myself if you keep me in a box?"

"I'm sorry, honey. You're right. We should have trusted you. But I'm trying to rectify that now."

"So this priest, he must be the one who kidnapped Seth."

"That's right."

"What are we doing sitting here? Let's go after him!"

Duncan jumped up, pounding his meaty fist into his meaty palm. "Yeah, Harold is gonna get Dunc'd."

I smiled.

"Love the enthusiasm, Duncan, but let's defeat evil

without resorting to catch phrases."

Mom didn't seem to notice. She looked at her lap.

"I can't go."

"What? What are you talking about? My boyfriend has been kidnapped by an evil priest named Harold and you're not going to help me?"

"I can't. Harold put an incantation on me so I can't go within 100 miles of him. Kind of like a magical restraining order."

"So magic is real?"

"Just as it relates to mummies."

"Should have assumed. But so what? You've got magic too! You don't have to listen to his magic."

"You can't violate a magical restraining order, Princess. Besides, he knows my weaknesses too well, I wouldn't be much help."

I sighed loudly. "This guy is a real asshole."

"Actually, I deserved the restraining order."

"What?"

"Never mind. But don't worry, I'm going to help you the only way I can. Harold and his grave robbers still think I have the River Jewel, so I'm going to distract them."

She pulled an identical necklace out of her bag and put it on. I looked sideways at it.

"It's a duplicate, honey. No power but it looks the same. They'll chase me all over and if they catch me, it won't do them any good. Meanwhile, you and Duncan sneak in and rescue Seth."

"I just got you back, and you're leaving."

"Technically, *you're* leaving. The Priest is hiding out in Alexandria, building an army to eventually overthrow the world, and you're leaving to stop him. And, of course, rescue Seth."

I wasn't sure I was ready for this, but Mom hugged us and pushed us toward the door.

"Wear a coat, honey."

"It's Egypt in summer. It's gonna be hot."

"I know. I just haven't gotten to be your mother in a while. Be safe, Princess."

In the parking lot, Duncan broke our silence.

"There's something about this that doesn't quite scan for me. If The Priest is after the Jewel, why did he send grave robbers to attack you? Did he think you had it?"

"I don't know."

"And why doesn't your mom just throw it in the ocean or something so it can't fall into the wrong hands? And how is he going to build an army by healing people?"

"Still don't know."

"And how is Seth involved in all this? What's his role?"

"Let me check real quick—nope, I don't know."

"Sorry, Princess. I'm just grappling with this whole thing and even though I like your mom, I'm not sure she's telling you the whole truth."

"Me too, Duncan. I'm new to love and short on trust, so I'm not sure I can assign either to my mom at the moment. But I want to so badly."

To tell the truth, I wasn't sure about Seth either. He was sent to kidnap my mom but fell in love with me instead? That's not a good start to a relationship.

Chapter 14

Flights to Alexandria are expensive. Really really expensive. Who knew?

I had a little money saved up from allowances and odd jobs, but Duncan, it turned out, had a pile of it he was going to use to finance his dig next summer. I didn't ask him to use it. Honestly I didn't. He insisted.

"We're pursuing a mummy and stopping grave robbers. That's definitely in the spirit of the Dig Fund."

"I'll pay you back, I promise."

"You're part goddess. I'm sure money isn't going to be a problem for you forever."

"If you ever need a thousand cats, I know a guy."

The conversation with my Dad went even better.

"So Dad," I said over a plate of eggs WAY over hard, "I'm thinking of taking a trip to Alexandria."

"Okay."

"Leaving tonight."

"Sure. Virginia or Egypt?"

"Egypt."

"Hot there this time of year. Virginia too, for that matter."

"To save my boyfriend from an evil Priest."

"Huh. That sounds noble of you."

"He is kind of a mummy."

"Ah, I guess that makes sense. All the bandages and stuff. I thought it was a hipster thing."

"You're taking this awfully well," I said.

"You're an adult, honey, and you'll have to learn to make your own mistakes."

"I'm 17," I corrected.

"Ah, right. Well, you're a teenager and you'll have to learn to make your own mistakes."

"Also, I saw Mom."

That caught him and he paused, mid-bite, then swallowed. He didn't look up.

"How'd she look?"

"Good," I said honestly. "Really good."

"She miss us?"

"Of course."

"Is she coming back?" he said, trying not to sound too hopeful.

"Honestly, I don't know."

"Well, she's an adult. She gets to make her own mistakes too."

He tried so hard to seem confident around me, but I could tell this was really hard for him.

"But you're coming back, right?"

"Definitely," I said, and put an arm around his shoulder. "I promise."

"Good. Gonna be lonely around here without you. Have to make lots of pie."

"That's a good idea."

"Need money?" I shook my head. "Duncan going with you?" I nodded. "Got your Mace?" I nodded again.

As much as we wanted to, we couldn't bring Khu on the flight with us. The conversation had gone something like this:

"We're going on the plane to Alexandria now."

Silence.

"You can't come."

A tilt of his magnificent head and sharp beak.

"But we'll meet up in Alexandria, okay?"

He let out a cluck that could only be described as a grumble as he realized how long the flight was going to be for him.

I nudged Duncan's arm. He produced a couple of small fish from his backpack. Khu nodded and ate the fish whole, then shot me a dirty look.

"Hey, I don't make FAA regulations," I said, but before I could finish he was in the air, probably figuring he'd get a head start on us.

Dad dropped us at the curb of the airport. He looked like he was going to make a speech, then thought better of it and hugged us both at the same time, leaning in to kiss me on the forehead.

"See you in a bit," he said. Then, after a pause, "thanks for telling me where you're going. And thanks in advance for coming back."

"Of course, Dad."

At the gate we had an hour to kill, which was too much

time to think. I paced nervously around a magazine stand. I picked up a magazine and then threw it back down.

"Calm down, Princess. Your fight is with The Priest, not *Men's Health*."

"It's not even the fight, though I'm terrified of that too."

"What is it?"

"I'm not sure I can tell you."

Sigh. "It's about Seth then?"

I nodded.

"Look, I've decided to keep being your friend even though you destroyed my heart, so you're going to have to talk to me about this eventually."

We walked along the terminal, and I pretended I was really interested in the food options. He let me take my time starting the conversation. Finally, I decided I was ready to open up to him.

"If my family didn't have the River Jewel, Seth would never have fallen in love with me."

"You mean fallen in *like*, right?"

"Yeah, that."

"We don't get to pick who we love. Or like. Otherwise I'd pick somebody who thought mummies were better in tombs than in bed."

I slapped his arm. "It'd be easier if you didn't think about me that way."

"Exactly my point. We can't choose. And regardless of what causes you to meet somebody in the first place, if your 'like' is real, it's because of who you actually are. It's possible he's just pretending to like you to steal the Jewel, but I doubt I'm that lucky."

He smiled. I hugged him.

"Thank you for going on an international flight to certain death with me, Duncan."

"Don't mention it."

We used even more of Duncan's dig money to pay for the WiFi on the first leg of our flight so I could do the only thing that calmed my nerves: research. I combed through every document I could download (painfully slowly) about Alexandria, mummification, curses, magic spells generally, and priestly incantations specifically.

After a few hours I was pretty sure I could perform a mummification from memory if given the proper equipment and, of course, a dead thing. Seth, being royalty, would have undergone the most thorough version of the process, while normal people were given a much more cursory preservation. I made a note to ask Seth about the specifics of his process and hoped him being dead at the time didn't dull his memories. It's a fascinating procedure.

Obviously they hadn't removed his brain through his nose because he's so smart. Or maybe the ritual to bring him back to life included a part where you have to put a new brain in. Does it go in through the nose too? Every question I answered raised three more. Did magic-ing him back to life fix everything or just animate what was there?

Maybe I'd do some field research on his body when Seth and I were alone. Ugh, why am I making everything gross?

I went back to researching as fast as satellite internet would allow. When I'm Googling, sometimes I can actually hit a zone where the whole world fades away and it just feels like knowledge is washing over me. It's probably like what it feels like to play sports. Some day I'll Google sports.

And now a brief break for Sofia's Mummy Minute, brought to you by The Internet.

There used to be a lot of mummies traveling the world. Not walking around kissing people, but preserved corpses taken out of Egypt by tourists. Rich people who traveled there could just buy mummies as souvenirs and then put them on display in private homes or used as the center-piece of "unwrapping parties." And if that wasn't weird enough, the preserved bodies were frequently ground up into medicine and pigments for painters. Humans can be so disrespectful: mummies are not playthings; they should be held and cuddled and loved.

This concludes Sofia's Mummy Minute, brought to you by The Internet. The Internet: are you sure you want to know the answer to that question?

After I ran out of information about mummies, I dove into restraining orders, in case there was something to learn there. In my proudest moment, I was able to find ac-tual text of a "schism spell" that creates a rift in space and time that cannot be crossed. This must have been what The Priest used on my mom. It was more steps than I expected. Mom must have really pissed this guy off.

There was an antidote spell, but where would I get river water and the intestines of 15 fresh-water fish in time to break the schism? There was no way mom would be able to join us on this fight.

Then I started creating the biggest possible family tree. To get back to ancient Egypt we're talking about 100 gen-erations, give or take. Since the family always had exactly one daughter, it didn't branch out of control, but I still had space for 100+ demigods. The joy of genealogy distracted me from my fear of death for at least a couple hours. Dun-can worked on a People Magazine crossword puzzle which, since he has a brain, must have been really depressing.

Next, we focused on the difficult task of actually finding The Priest. Together, Duncan and I poured over maps of Alexandria, trying to figure out where an evil mastermind would set up camp.

"I just had a thought," Duncan said suddenly. "Seth was somehow involved with this guy, so The Priest probably set up camp near the tomb Seth was buried in. We'll start with some of the Macedonian tombs and work our way back to ones from the Ptolemaic Period. I'm expecting it'll be one of those, judging by how well preserved he is."

I smiled at him and he beamed. It felt for a moment like we'd actually be able to do this, then I remembered we'd have to fight. We took inventory of our strengths. My brief experiment with the martial arts might help. Duncan, despite his size, didn't have any fighting skills. He had all his archeological tools in his bag, so if we needed to painstakingly dig anything up, he'd be ready. And he was great at miniature golf.

We were screwed.

We decided stealth would be our best option. If we found The Priest, we'd scope the situation, sneak in, and rescue Seth in a surgical strike.

And then run.

Once we were over the ocean and the WiFi crapped out, we tried to take our minds off our impending doom. We picked out our favorite items from Skymall, then we got bored and watched the mummy movie Duncan had loaded up on his laptop. It just didn't capture the subtle sexiness of a real mummy. The dusty allure, the gaunt beauty, the hoodie.

When we landed, we quickly discovered that all the planning, the stress, and the research was all useless. The Priest was kind enough to have a group of grave robbers meet us at the airport, knock us out, and take us directly to the tomb he'd set up as his base of operations. I'd love to say we put up a good fight, but we definitely did not.

In our defense, there were a lot of them. And they blended in with the throng of taxi drivers trying to get the attention of arriving tourists. And we were really jet lagged. And without the cats, we were badly outnumbered.

Chapter 15

"I didn't want to die, obviously, but I tried to look on the bright side: my death would save the people I loved the most, Dad, Mom, Duncan, and *him*. Him. I loved him, I knew that now. Plus I wouldn't have to go to Trig on Monday."

One of the grave robbers splashed water from a bucket onto my face and I opened my eyes.

"Stop being so damn dramatic, Princess," said a man in a simple khaki robe, tied at the waist.

"Aw, hell. Was that out loud?" I was tied to a chair in a dark, stone room. "Great."

"When people wake up from being knocked out, they have a tendency to talk to themselves," offered Eli. "Guy back in Oslo couldn't stop describing the light coming from the bare light bulb. It was damned poetic if you ask me."

"Breathtaking," said Bunny. "It must've been a crime, what we did to him."

"It was literally a crime, yes." Eli said knowledgeably. "Or more accurately a collection of crimes."

"Not to mention the conspiracy to commit those crimes

which is itself a crime," offered the robe man.

The grave robbers nodded thoughtfully.

"Excuse me, guys. I've never been kidnapped before so I didn't know how it would affect me. And now that I'm awake, I don't care what you do to me, because it's all true. I love him. And even if you kill me, you'll never find him."

The one in the robe laughed.

"Um, have you forgotten that we kidnapped him and used him as bait to lure you here in the first place? We must have concussed you worse than I thought. My apologies."

"Aw, nuts."

"Besides, he's my creation. I could find him anywhere."

"What are you talking about? Who are you?" I leaned forward to get a better look. The old wooden chair wobbled.

"Careful, Princess," said the man. "Stone floors are uneven, and awfully firm. I'd hate for you to fall and break a wrist or something."

"What do you mean you created Seth?" I demanded.

"Come on, Princess. Don't be so naive. Mummies don't just get up and start walking around on their own. It requires days of preparation, hours of a very precise ritual, plus some pretty obscure ingredients. You spend days shopping..." He sounded wistful. "Seth was my first attempt, when I was a much younger Priest. He was beautiful and while I consider him my greatest success, he was my only mistake. The revival went better than I could have dreamed, but something went wrong during the control prayers. All his brothers serve me without question but he has a mind of his own."

"You're Harold!"

"No!" He snapped. "I'm The Priest. Harold is dead."

"Okay, sure, Harold."

Bunny and Eli snickered until Harold shot them a look and they straightened up.

"I bet that makes you feel like a big man, forcing people to follow you." I spat at him.

With words, I mean. It was too dusty in this cramped stone room to get any real spit going. And while I was terrified, I wasn't nervous so my saliva hurricane wasn't active at the moment.

"I just love your spirit, Princess. Even fierier than your mom. I bet your heart has a bright, gamey taste to it."

"Ugh, gross."

"Don't knock it, my dear," he said. "If you're lucky, I may give you a bite."

This was getting a bit too real, and I was desperate. "Duncan will save me!"

He laughed out loud. I would have assumed it'd be an ominous laugh, but his was reedy and must really grate on people at the movies.

"Obviously, I'm not going to untie you so you can see him, but rest assured your precious Duncan is as incapacitated as you are. He's been crying a lot in his sleep. Not what I expect from a big guy like that, but you really can't judge a book by it's cover, now can you?"

"That could be the steroids."

"Ah, well, that would explain it. They really aren't worth it."

"We agree on that, at least."

"Anyway, in conclusion, nobody is going to save you, and you are going to die. It's just you and me, my dear."

Bunny cleared his throat.

"And my goons."

Bunny nodded his appreciation. I glowered at them.

No problem. I can still be defiant, even if I'll die soon.

"But you'll never find the River Jewel!"

The Priest rubbed his hand over his face. "Jesus, you really have no idea what you're a part of, do you?" He held up the necklace. "If you knew how powerful this was, you wouldn't have kept it in your jacket pocket."

"Aw, damn it! I'm so bad at this."

"Don't be so hard on yourself, Princess. This is your first rodeo. I, on the other hand, have been going to rodeos like this for years. Decades of rodeos, really. When your mom left with the Jewel, I had lots of time to prepare for its inevitable return. And now that I have it and you, it's the small matter of actually completing the incantations and then my mummy army will rise and do my bidding. I'll be unstoppable. The world will quake in terror. It will be my greatest rodeo of all!"

"Well, I'm sure something will go wrong with your stupid army rodeo thing. It's too complicated of a plan to go off without a hitch."

"Ah, but it isn't that complicated. It's this stone that makes all my work possible. The river gives life; the River Jewel has that power condensed. With it, I can resurrect hordes of the dead."

"But the Jewel only works if you have the blood of Anuket in your veins."

"And that's why you're here. You seem like you've got plenty of blood in you. I'll inject a little bit at a time into my veins and then I'll be able to complete all the rituals."

"Super double triple crap!" I fell for his trap hook, line, and Duncan. I chased Seth here and brought the two things he needed. I was like Amazon for evil ingredients.

Now all I could hope to do was stall him. Maybe if I filibustered, he'd get tired and put off raising the dead and taking over the world for a couple days.

"A blue rock can do that? That's pretty cool." Great

work, mouth. Another home run for team Beige.

He shrugged. "It also helps me live forever. And you can use it to divine the best location for a well. Probably lots of other stuff, but I've got eternity to figure out all its off-label uses."

As much as I hated The Priest, he was the first person who'd actually been kind enough to explain things to me clearly. Credit where credit's due: he was an asshole, but at least he didn't start a bunch of sentences and then stop them.

I tried another ploy.

"And that's why you kidnapped my mom. You bastard."

"What? No, Princess. Does nobody tell you anything?"

"Seriously, nobody does."

He kept talking while he meticulously rearranged a table full of terrifying looking instruments and average looking jars. My filibuster wasn't really working. It was more like I was keeping him company.

"Well then this one's gonna be hard to take, but I didn't kidnap your mom. She came to me and asked for a job. I needed an assistant and she seemed reliable, so I hired her. Nothing evil about it, just a college graduate looking for entry level work."

"What? That doesn't make sense. Why would she come all the way here?"

"She was young and looking for excitement. She came to Egypt hoping to teach English but didn't find a job. Plus I created a spell that acted as a beacon for Anuket's descendents, so that helped too."

"And then you forced her into your evil schemes, you monster."

"No no no.. Calm down, princess. I just employed her. Things were going great and then she had to go and fall in love with me and ruin everything."

"You're insane."

"I'm evil. Let's not complicate this by stigmatizing mental illness."

"A fair point. But there's no way my mom fell in love with an evil man."

"She did!" he said, suddenly defensive. "I told her I wanted to just stay coworkers and she freaked out. She called every five minutes, she followed me around, she actually lit my car on fire. It was scary! Sure, that could have had something to do with the spell, but still. My car! Jesus. That's why I had to put a magic restraining order on her. I heard she ran back to America to start a family and settle down, and good riddance. Seriously, I haven't seen her since the '70s."

My head was spinning. There were lots of factors: his revelation, the concussion I recently suffered, fear of death, and even some jet lag still. But mostly, it was his revelation.

"Admittedly, I used her fondness for me to convince her to donate blood to my cause and overlook some of the fringier sides of my business."

"Like raising an army of mummies to take over the world."

"That kind of stuff, yeah. Her blood was crucial to that. It took me decades to perfect the process and I lost several wonderful specimens along the way. Two years ago I started seeing some success."

"Seth."

"That's right, you've met him. He was the first one to completely reanimate. Then I ran out of her blood and I had to get your mom back. That's why I started sending search parties like Bunny and Eli."

"That's why she left! She figured out you were looking for her, and she went into hiding!"

"Apparently. After several years of fruitless searching, I sent in Seth and he discovered you instead and suddenly he stopped responding to my commands. The whole thing's become quite a debacle, honestly. An ugly mark on my career. But I won't make that mistake again. This time I'm going to skip the whole interpersonal relationship and just cut your heart out and keep all your blood in jars. That way I can use it whenever I need without somebody telling me how much she admires me for living my dream. Your mom is a sweet woman, really, but she is terrible at reading people."

"I know the feeling."

Somewhere in the dusty tomb, Duncan groaned.

"Just a moment, Duncan," said The Priest. He bowed to me. "If you'll excuse me, Princess. I must tend to our other guest. I'm thinking I'll kill him, mummify him, then bring him back as one of my soldiers. A guy that big is sure to come in handy."

"No!" I yelled after The Priest as he left the room.

Then I heard another sound. It wasn't a passed out Duncan. It was the shuffling of incredibly sexy bandaged-wrapped feet!

"Whoa there, you stay put," said Bunny.

"Seth, you're here too! Why didn't you say something?"

His feet shuffled some more.

"He's gagged, Princess," Eli informed me. "If you keep asking all these questions we're going to have to gag you too. Harold, er, The Priest is a good guy and a visionary leader, but he gets sidetracked so easily."

Bunny nodded. "He's more of an artist than a producer, you know?"

I craned my neck, and I could just make out the edge of Seth's hoodie.

Eli looked a bit sad. He rolled his eyes, then walked over

to Seth. "Fine, lovebirds. You should get to say your last goodbyes."

Bunny protested, then sighed. "Yeah, I guess so."

Seth inhaled deeply as his gag was removed. "Sofia!"

"Seth!"

"I'm so sorry!"

"Me too! This is a terrible rescue!"

"No kidding. Worst I've ever received."

"Hey, I may be tied up but I can still hear your tone, mister."

"I'm sorry I couldn't tell you everything sooner. I hoped I could avoid this kind of violent showdown by keeping you in the dark. I see now that this was the inevitable result of any relationship that lacks communication. Just stay calm and after we escape this, I'll be more open about my feelings and my needs. Promise."

"I'm sure that would sound great if I wasn't about to get murdered and canned, rendering this whole thing moot. Not that there's anything wrong with being dead per se. You wear it very well."

"Thanks, I guess."

A scuffle in the other room caught Bunny and Eli's attention, and they left to investigate.

Seth hushed his voice, "Quick, scoot back to me. I think I can untie your ropes and then you can untie mine. When they come back we'll rush them, grab the Jewel, and escape together."

"Yes!"

In my excitement, I scooted my chair too fast and felt the balance shift. I toppled over backward, slamming back into the stone floor and shrouding my whole world in darkness.

Chapter 16

As I swam in my second concussion of the day, I had
a vision that I was back at The Red Roof Inn, room #419.
Inside was the sound of a celebration. As I opened the door,
I saw Seth and my mom high fiving while Duncan playfully rubbed Khu's plumage. Everybody was celebrating the
amazing victory they'd just had over evil while I was tied
to a chair and unconscious.

"It's over?" I stammered. "I missed the whole thing?"

"Did you see the part where your mom burst into the
room shooting jets of water out of her eyes?"

"No!"

"Then yeah, you missed the whole thing."

"Oh God damn it!" I said.

"Yeah, I'd be pissed too," said Duncan. "I can't imagine how I'd feel about myself if I hadn't used my intimate
knowledge of archeology to turn the tide of the battle and
save everyone. It was a real confidence booster for me."

"That was the best," said Seth, admiringly.

"You weren't bad yourself, Seth. You must have cursed

15 grave robbers single-handedly with that magical staff you pulled out of nowhere."

"Well, thank you. But we know who the real hero is."

Khu clucked, and my mom tossed him a fish.

They all laughed.

"So I really did nothing?" I asked.

"Well, Bunny almost tripped over you when he was running away from Duncan," said Seth.

"He didn't, though," said my mom.

"No," agreed Seth, "he was fine."

"But it's okay," Duncan said placatingly. "We were there to protect you."

"We always protect you," said Seth.

Mom nodded. "Speaking of which, we got you this beautiful plastic bubble to live inside."

Seth agreed. "It's the safest place for you."

Duncan chimed in, "And we'll all stand around the bubble at all times, making sure nothing comes near it."

"And if anything pops the bubble," my mom added, "I can use this to fix it." She held up the River Jewel.

I grasped at my own necklace. She laughed.

"You didn't think I gave you the real one, did you? That's so silly. Yours is the duplicate."

Everybody laughed, but Khu's laugh felt the meanest.

I woke up screaming.

Bunny and Eli jogged back in.

"Jesus, Princess. How did you manage to hurt yourself even after we tied you up?"

"The Priest is going to kill you; you don't need to do it yourself."

I groaned, my splitting headache returning. They righted my chair and pushed it against a wall so I couldn't fall backwards again.

"Please take care of yourself for just one more minute, Princess. Duncan is being a real pain right now." Eli said, before leaving the room again with Bunny by his side.

Before Seth and I could start planning our escape again, a skinny figure emerged from a dark corner of the room. I almost screamed again when I recognized Khu, but I held back.

"I could kiss you right now! I forgive you for being a jerk in my dream."

Khu cocked his head.

"Do you have a plan, my friend?" Seth asked the bird, in what I thought was an optimistic delegation of responsibility.

Khu continued to stare at us, confused. Then he straightened up, seeming pleased with himself for finding us. He looked between us for a fish or frog to reward him for his long journey.

"Well, I guess we're done." Seth said. "Even your mom can't save us at this point."

"No, she's got a schism spell on her and OH GOD I HAVE A PLAN."

"Seriously, keep your voice down, Princess. You're terrible at this."

"Sorry. It's my first rodeo. Okay, on the plane I figured out that the spell works by creating a schism in space and time."

"Sure, a schism spell."

"But we've got the River Jewel. It's right there on the table!"

Slowly Seth figured out what I was thinking. "It fixes things that're broken so you're going to--"

"Fix the schism in space and time! Then mom can come help us."

I hummed the four notes my mom had and stared intently at the River Jewel. The air seemed to shudder a bit but nothing happened.

We both waited for a second to see if anything would change. Nothing did.

"Did it work?"

"No idea."

Khu looked at us angrily. We still hadn't given him any fish. He harrumphed, then hopped back into the darkness.

"It's okay, Sofia. It takes a while to get the hang of controlling a jewel like that."

"So we're back to being screwed because of my incompetence."

Bunny, Eli, and The Priest came back in before we could try any more bright ideas.

"That guy sure is a handful," The Priest said, wiping his hands on his robe. Bunny was dragging the chair with Duncan in it. He was snoring loudly.

"Did you knock him out?" I said, scared for all of us with these concussions. "After you take all our blood, you should at least donate our brains to science for CTE research."

"What?"

"Never mind."

"I didn't hit him, if that's what you're implying. I gave him an Ambien. And that's all the preparation I can do for today. The spell requires me to sit in a sauna of purifying smoke for 12 hours before I can start the ritual and for you to fast for at least that long, so I'm off to turn into a smelly prune while you get good and hungry." He laughed his reedy laugh to himself.

"What's funny about that?"

"A smelly prune, Princess. That's a funny image." Bunny and Eli tried to join him in a chuckle but clearly didn't mean it.

"Is it? You've been too busy trying to overthrow the world's governments to learn the structure of jokes," I said grumpily.

"Enough. Save your energy for tomorrow. You have some very important bleeding out to do." He grabbed his robe and stormed out of the room.

Bunny gagged Seth and me, blew out the candles, and left. I heard the sound of scraping stones locking us in our dusty prison. We were enclosed in darkness and, more literally, 3 feet of ancient rock. Even if we somehow got untied, we'd never be able to move the stones.

I cried softly, wishing The Priest had offered me an Ambien too.

For hours I drifted in and out of consciousness. My nightmares alternated between being killed by The Priest and being rescued from The Priest only to be forced into a bubble by the people I loved the most. I wasn't sure which would be worse at this point. Well, okay. Being killed was clearly worse, but the elapsed time hadn't made me any less dramatic, and I was sick of feeling useless.

Eventually the sound of giant stones scraping against each other indicated that The Priest and his fellow assholes were returning. I expected a match to flare up, lighting the ceremonial candles to signal my imminent de-blooding, but instead I was blinded by the harsh white light of a phone being used as flashlight.

"RRwardgraw rdart grwnwnr?" I yelled into my gag.

"Sofia?"

"Mrhrrm?"

"Shhhhhh. You'll wake the dead if you keep that up.

Nothing personal, Seth."

"Mrphe hrphfm" he said.

"Would you two be quiet?" she yell-whispered. "Seri-ously. It's like this is your first rodeo."

She pulled the gag out of my mouth then started work-ing on my hands.

"It basically is, Mom," I said as soon as I could talk. My voice came out dry and raspy. "And I've never been to a rodeo either, but I think I'd like it about as much as being kidnapped and ritualistically murdered."

"Are you finished, young lady?"

"Yes. Now you talk. How are you here??"

"The strangest thing. Khu showed up at my hotel and tried to drag me out with his beak."

A clucking sound in the darkness told me Khu was here with her, and I started crying again.

"Harold must have lifted the restraining order because I came here straight away and nothing stopped me."

"It worked! I used the Jewel to heal the space/time schism."

She pulled back and looked at me, stunned. "My God, Princess Sofia. How did you get so clever?"

"Good blood? Hard work? Google?"

She hugged me hard, then went back to untying our bonds. She managed to get the knots off my hands and waist, and we worked on my feet together.

"But Mom, that flight took us 28 hours. Did you teleport or something?"

"You flew commercial? Sorry, I should have told you the River Jewel can do a lot more than just fix stuff. For example, if you do it right you can create a funnel of water that will surf you anywhere in the world in about 15 min-utes. It's great. Just make sure you get a waterproof case for your phone and always pack a towel."

"Wait, if I had the real River Jewel, how did you use it?"

"They're both real."

"Why did you lie to me about that? I don't see how it even helped."

She sighed. "Force of habit, I guess. I've been on the run for a while."

We freed Seth, and he and I embraced quickly. We had all started on Duncan's bonds when we heard voices outside.

"Shit. Shit shit shit."

"Language, young lady."

"Cluck!" yelled Khu.

Seth shushed all three of us and then Mom stood up and whispered.

"Let me handle this. I know Harold better than any of you. I can talk him into taking my blood instead."

"No!"

"Yes, Sofia. Let me handle this."

"Nope. We don't have time for you to try to shield me, Mom. We're all getting out of this and I know how. Our only advantage right now is surprise, right? Mom, Khu, they don't know you're here. Hide behind those tables. Duncan, Seth and I are going to pretend to still be tied up. When they come in, I'll give the signal, and we'll rush him. We've got one chance at this."

Everybody stared at me stunned.

"Now!" I whisper-yelled at them.

The voices were getting closer. Mom and Khu disappeared into the shadows, and Seth and I sat back down and put our hands behind our backs. In the dim light there was no way for the grave robbers to tell we were free. Duncan was still tied at the ankles and waist and he was gagged, so he wasn't going to be much help.

A match flared and lit a large candle on the altar, then two more. In the dim light I could make out The Priest, now in a darker robe and flanked by a tired-looking Bunny and Eli.

Behind them shuffled a mummy holding a ceremonial pillow with my River Jewel on it. Like Seth, the new mummy was graceful and sexy, but he was bigger and meaner too. I hated him immediately.

"Good morning, Princess. Gentlemen."

I mumbled, pretending I was sleepy and confused. Bunny came up to me.

"What happened to your gag?"

"I must have chewed through it."

"Gross."

"Not the grossest thing that happened last night. Hard to pee when you're tied up like this."

He retreated immediately, wanting nothing to do with this part of false imprisonment.

"Well, are you ready, my dear?" The Priest turned toward me.

"Ugh, you smell awful. I can't believe I'm going to be killed by a stinkpile."

"Is that supposed to hurt my feelings? I was in a purifying smoke for several hours, the smell is part of the effect."

He took a step in my direction. Just a little bit further now...

"Now I know to you this seems like I'm exsanguinating you because I'm a gigantic asshole. But you really should think of it as your chance to sacrifice yourself for something greater."

I needed to draw him out a tiny bit more.

"Nothing about you is greater than me. In fact, you're

lesser. If there was a giant greater-than symbol here right now, the proper place to put it would be between me and you with the big, open side pointing at me. And sure, it'd just look like a giant arrow to most people, but you and I would know what it was really for."

I'd never been prouder of my word vomit.

He cocked his head and looked at me quizzically. He took another step forward. One more and he'd be in range.

"Did you know when I get nervous, I salivate? It's probably going to ruin your whole experiment."

"What are you even talking about anymore?"

I opened my mouth wide like he was a dentist.

He stepped once more towards me and bent over to peer into my mouth. I gathered all the anger of the last 10 years. The pain of my mother leaving, the pain it caused my dad. Seth disappearing. Hurting Duncan. And other stuff, stuff that wasn't even The Priest's fault. The time I got a C on a math test for not showing my work even though I got the right answers. Everything was at a breaking point and all that rage built up in my right leg and pushed into my knee, which I drove up and into The Priest's balls like a crash test car hitting a brick wall at 40 miles per hour.

He screamed and fell to the ground clutching himself, rolling around in the fetal position, and then vomited. I vowed to send Punchy Jim flowers when I got home.

The mummy dropped the pillow and the Jewel crashed to the stone floor, shattering.

I heard my mom's voice from the darkness. "I'm going to assume that was the signal."

"Yes! Signal! Now! This is the signal!" I shouted.

Bunny, Eli, and the mummy spun around, not sure where the sound was coming from.

Seth grabbed the bad mummy and grappled him to the ground. If I had more time, I might have found it erotic. Or maybe not, this was all pretty new for me.

Mom rushed toward the Jewel, humming.

Khu rushed at Eli and started pecking at his face. Eli grabbed the bird's noble neck and tried to hold him back.

Duncan apparently wasn't willing to sit this whole thing out, because he stood up, still attached to the chair, turned his back toward Bunny, then quickly backed up. The legs of the chair pinned Bunny against the wall. Although he struggled, Duncan's bulk was enough to completely incapacitate him.

"This is for the mini golf course, you son of a bitch," Duncan said, meaner than I'd ever heard him.

Mom looked like she was going to toss me the reconstituted River Jewel but then thought better of it and darted to me and handed it off. We looked around and decided Khu needed the most help. We each grabbed an arm and tried to pull Eli off Khu, who continued his pecking onslaught undaunted. Even with two of us, though, Eli's massive arms were too strong.

Khu gestured toward the floor and I looked down. His brilliantly colored leg pushed a small metal can my way. Mace!

I grabbed the can and sprayed it directly into Eli's mouth, and he collapsed. Mom used the rope from Seth and wrapped it around Eli as the bulky graverobber coughed and sputtered. As she did, I hummed the notes of the River Jewel and directed its power to repair the frayed ends of the rope, binding it seamlessly around him, making it impossible for him to move his upper body. Khu climbed onto his chest and stood majestically, pinning him to the ground.

I surveyed my troops. I hadn't expected us to gain the upper hand so quickly, but this could still slip away from us at any moment. The thorough Macing we'd given Eli came at a cost, though. The terrible ventilation in the tomb meant that we were all starting to choke on peppery fumes.

The Priest was still on the ground covered in his own vomit and holding himself, but he managed to mumble something under his breath. Suddenly the passageway erupted with the clatter of weapons and the sounds of fragile feet dragging themselves along the stone floor.

"My sons and daughters," The Priest squeaked out, his voice even higher than usual, "destroy these interlopers."

Eyes burning, I looked up to see the first of what appeared to be dozens, maybe hundreds, of mummies carrying spears and axes. One even had a chain like an 80s biker gang. We were badly outnumbered and outgunned.

"What do we do now?" I said. "I'm not in charge anymore."

My mom grabbed my hand.

"How well do you swim?"

"Um?"

She quickly recited four ancient words over and over while holding her duplicate Jewel in one hand and my trembling hand in the other.

Somewhere far off I could hear a rushing, gurgling sound. It got steadily louder.

"Oh God. Seth!"

I dropped my mom's hand and rushed to where the bad mummy had pinned Seth's arm in some kind of wrestling hold and was threatening to break it off. I kicked Bad Mummy in the chest, and my foot went halfway through him like I'd kicked a down pillow. He crumpled, and I pulled Seth up and lifted him over my head. What remained of his body had shockingly little weight and I was able to hold him there with ease, inches from the ceiling.

As I did, river water flooded into the chamber, immediately up to our waists. The mummy army's lower halves disintegrated and they collapsed into the water. If I didn't hurry, the same would surely happen to Seth.

The water was still rising and I was on the verge of panic. The humans in the chamber were splashing and yelling, the pepper still searing my eyes and lungs, Seth above me yelling instructions. I looked around for help.

"Go!" my mom yelled above the roar of the water. "Get out of here now."

I used my last mental energy to focus on the light coming from the exit, and I pushed hard against the current in that direction. Every ounce of strength I'd built from skipping P.E. slipped out of my body as we burst through the opening into the blinding morning sun. I scampered up the side of the stone of the burial temple we'd just left and set Seth down gently on the top.

"You saved me," Seth said, the fear not fully gone from his voice. "That water would have--"

"I have to go back for them."

"No. Just wait. Your mom knows water."

"But Duncan."

"He'll be--"

Just then, the water reversed, shooting out the small doorway as if the whole temple were doing a spit take.

A pile of wet bodies were sprinkled over the desert, and they struggled to find their feet as the water soaked into the sand. Mom was the only one standing confidently, while Duncan squirmed, still attached to his chair. Eli struggled with his rope but made no progress and Bunny choked and coughed up brackish water. Khu was unfazed, happily munching on a couple of fish left flopping on dry land, completely unaware of the mess they'd gotten tangled up in.

Seth looked around dejectedly. Pieces of gauze were scattered everywhere, like somebody had toilet-papered the desert. It was gruesome.

Everybody was so dazed, it was several minutes before anybody noticed The Priest was nowhere to be found. After securing the other prisoners, we cautiously ventured back into the temple, but all we found was his ceremonial robe. That made me feel a little better, I guess; whether he escaped by magic, was hiding in a secret passageway in the temple, or had simply ducked out and ran when we weren't looking, I was glad to know he was doing it naked. I hoped that was super awkward for him.

Chapter 17

Of all the indignities I'd suffered in my life, probably the greatest one was having to go back to school after saving the world.

For weeks it took all my self control not to write, "You don't seem to appreciate what I did for you" on all my homework assignments.

There were plenty of good parts of life getting back to a semblance of normalcy. Seth, for one. Okay, Seth for most of them.

But other things too. My mom wasn't really back to being my mom full time, but she and dad were feeling things out, and it was going pretty well. They went on a couple of dates and while their relationship couldn't move fast enough for me, I was already noticing plenty of changes at home. Once Dad accidentally underbaked chocolate chip cookies to a golden brown and let me eat them anyway. Aside from not dying at the hands of a sociopathic magician, that was the greatest thing that happened to me all year.

I told Dad everything; he deserved that at least. He hung on my every word and couldn't hear enough about me nut-kicking Harold or Macing Eli into oblivion. He also worried. A lot.

I went to multiple doctors to check for lasting damage from the concussions. I seemed to be in the clear there, but he also required me to start seeing a therapist in case I showed any lasting effects of the trauma I'd suffered.

Dr. Becky and I got along fine, though her overly serious demeanor and tiny glasses perched on her pointy nose made me giggle when she would prefer I didn't. We're working through that, as well as the fact that I was kidnapped and nearly murdered.

I also decided early on that she could help me deal with the trauma of the kidnapping without needing to know the whole thing about mummies and magic. She'd worked too hard to understand the world one way for me to mess it all up, you know? I just said "my mom's ex-boyfriend" and she seemed comfortable with that.

What nobody talked about was The Priest. Did he survive? How? Where was he now? What was he doing? Was he still naked? If he had lived through it, he'd lost his army, both River Jewels, and all of Anuket's blood, so he couldn't just go reincarnating a mummy again. That was comforting, but he was still dangerous. Very dangerous.

As the months slid by, though, I wondered about it less and less. Maybe if I didn't think about him, he'd actually stay gone. Like fairies. Are fairies real? I made a note to ask Seth.

Epilogue

I keep having this dream. I'll tell Dr. Becky about it soon, I promise.

The Priest and my mom are resurrecting a body. Mumbling incantations, mixing foul ingredients, squinting to read the recipe from an ancient text, the smell of burning sage filling the air.

Also, there's an octopus eating pancakes in the corner, making conversation with Seth, who stares at it intently.

Seth is naked.

Look, I'd love to pretend he's not naked, but he is.

The important part is the resurrection. I can't take my eyes off my mom and The Priest, working together so well. She flits around, grabbing terrifying tools from his hand the moment he's done with them, handing him the next ingredient before he even asks for it.

The way my mom looks: this is her with her guard down. She's happy. She looks at The Priest with respect and more, with love. And to see him work it's not hard to understand why. There's a confidence and strength to every motion, like an Olympic swimmer cutting the water, except he's cutting, you know, a human body.

It's a little while before I notice the body they're working on is mine. I shudder.

A beautiful woman appears next me with jet black hair partially covered by a large crown of golden feathers. She's resplendent in silk robes that shimmer with a bluish tint. She holds an ankh, which looks kinda like a stick figure trying to give you a hug. Even with the crown, I tower over her.

"People were much smaller back then," she says, as if she can feel me judging her for her height.

She's Anuket, the Goddess of the Nile that I'm supposedly related to. I've read every word about her available in any language.

"Are you real?" I ask her.

"Who can say what is real?"

"Well, the point of my question was to establish that."

"Don't think I'm missing the tone here, young lady."

"I think you're real. You're mummy-adjacent, thus by the established rules, you're probably real."

"Agreed," she says and crosses her arms. "But this is a dream, so you'll have to take it all with a grain of salt."

"Is it a lucid dream? Can I control it? I wish to fly!"

I jump but land again, just like normal.

"What is lucidity? What is control?"

"Ugh, you're the worst."

She nudges me, and I notice that Seth is now slow dancing with the octopus. I feel a pang of jealousy.

It's then that I notice that Seth isn't a mummy. His bandages are gone, and instead he's a vibrant, living young man.

Who is super duper naked.

"Okay, let's hurry up with the insight from the ancients, Great Grandma. I have a long night of, um, interactive dreaming ahead of me."

The goddess Anuket guffaws. "Honey, I've seen your fantasies. Did nobody teach you about sex? It's really nothing like bowling."

I bristle. "My fantasies are just fine, thank you. I've Googled all the parts I'm interested in."

"Well something's getting lost in translation, sweetie. For one thing, I would lose the octopus."

"But you don't have to," says the octopus, winking.

"Can you just interpret this, oh great Anuket? Pretty please?"

She sighs. "Fine, fine. Don't think I don't have better things to do, too."

She starts pointing around the room.

"You're wondering if you could somehow become a mummy, so you'd be a better match for Seth. You're worried your mom was happier when she was younger and didn't have you to take care of. And as for that," she gestures at the octopus, "you're worried that everybody (or everything) has more to offer Seth than you do. Also you watched that video about octopuses last week and you thought they were pretty cool."

"That's some potent insight."

"I'm taking the complement, missy, but I never miss the tone. If you want a second opinion, call in Bastet. She thinks everything is about making kittens."

"Please continue."

"Watching people poke at your body is a metaphor for the male gaze, the way society is always prodding at you with their eyes, judging you. Obviously you're still worried that The Priest is out there and that he'll try to kill you again. And viewing your own death from afar? I think you stole that from *Tom Sawyer*."

"Oh yeah," I say. "Sophomore English. I don't think I ever finished it."

"Racism is bad. Now you don't have to."

"Isn't that *Huckleberry Finn*?"

"You may be right. Is *Tom Sawyer* the one about painting fences?"

"Yep."

"Huh. Anyway, I'm off. Enjoy your super weird imaginary sex."

"That's it?"

"I guess I could stay, but that would be weirder for everybody involved. Well, except for the cephalopod who seems down for whatever."

The octopus smiles broadly and starts rubbing where I imagine his nipples would be.

"Please, Anuket. What do I do? Where do I go? How can I stop The Priest once and for all? Do I even need to?"

"Oh, Princess. Why do you think you're going to get life advice from a sex nightmare?"

I try not to pout, but it happens.

"Fine, fine, my dearest Sofia. I'll say one thing. Petra is nice this time of year. Lots of interesting things going on there."

"What's going on there?"

She just smiles.

The octopus leans in to kiss Seth, and I scream.

Seth rubs my shoulder and whispers.

"It's okay, Princess. You're safe."

The real Seth. Not naked, not kissing an octopus, not really alive.

The early light peeks in from the creases of our tent. Even though I'm slightly taller, he's always big spoon so I don't accidentally crush his fragile bones while we're sleeping.

Somewhere outside, Duncan is sharing a tent with Nicole, the desk clerk from the hotel, and hopefully sleeping through all this. He's all tuckered out by a full day of exploring rock structures and boring everybody but Seth with his analysis of what might have happened here.

"I know where he's hiding."

"Where who's hiding, my darling?" Seth asks sleepily.

"The Priest."

"What?" He's sitting up now, fully awake.

"He's in Petra."

"How do you know that?"

"I know it."

"Okay, we'll go to Petra."

I look at him expectantly. "Yeah?"

"Yeah. I mean, not right now. But after this camping trip, sure. As long as you're there to keep me safe, I'll go anywhere."

I kiss him passionately, then hold his face in my hands and stare deeply into his eye-voids.

"I love you, Seth."

"I love you, Princess Sofia."

Then he wipes his mouth with his sleeve so my saliva doesn't ruin centuries of careful preservation.